THE HAND THAT FEEDS YOU

Mercedes Rosende

Translated by Tim Gutteridge

BITTER LEMON PRESS
LONDON

BITTER LEMON PRESS

First published in the United Kingdom in 2023 by
Bitter Lemon Press, 47 Wilmington Square, London WC1X OET

www.bitterlemonpress.com

First published in Spanish in 2019 as
QUÉ GANAS DE NO VERTE NUNCA MÁS
by Editorial Planeta S.A., Montevideo

© 2019, Mercedes Rosende
English translation © Tim Gutteridge, 2023

This translation of QUÉ GANAS DE NO VERTE NUNCA MÁS is
published by arrangement with Ampi Margini Literary Agency
and with the authorization of Mercedes Rosende.

A CIP record for this book is available from the British Library

ISBN 978-1-913394-745
eBook ISBN USC 978-1-913394-752
eBook ISBN ROW 978-1-913394-769

Bitter Lemon Press gratefully acknowledges the financial assistance of Programa IDA

Typeset by Tetragon, London
Printed and bound by the CPI Group (UK) Ltd, Croydon, CRO 4YY

I keep an eye out for malice growing
like someone caring for a bonsai, which will die
if you leave it alone for just one day.
My tiny tree of rage,
my bloodless guillotine,
the altar
to the bad person we all are.
In the dead calm
the echo of an eye for an eye lying in wait,
misshapen body of resentment,
crow perched on the branch of the funeral cypress,
awaiting
the cruel, joyful moment when we'll be at hand.

JOSÉ EMILIO PACHECO
"The Tree of Malice"

Translation by Katherine Hedeen and Víctor Rodríguez Núñez

On 6 September 1971, 111 Tupamaro guerrillas escaped from Punta Carretas Prison, through a tunnel and without firing a single shot. It was one of the largest breakouts in history, and became known as El Abuso. The event occupied a prominent role in Uruguayan popular culture, on a par with Ernesto Che Guevara's visit to the country in 1961, or the appearance of German cruiser *Admiral Graf Spee* in the Bay of Montevideo in 1939.

RAMIRO SANCHIZ, *La Diaria*

THE ESCAPE

Ursula doesn't hesitate: she pushes Luz into the mouth of the tunnel. They leave behind them the brightly lit stores, the colourful clothes, the television sets, a world full of people. There is just the sound of piped music and the voices of the crowd. But the fear hasn't disappeared. It clings to Ursula's clothes, permeates her sweat, constricts her throat. It's a strange fear, akin to vertigo, yet with a hint of forbidden pleasure.

The jaws of the tunnel close and the two women disappear into the most absolute darkness, the scene fades to black, the sound recedes. It's hard to imagine, in this world of ours so full of stimuli.

Luz cried a little at first, a few tears cutting her cheeks, but she's stopped now. Ursula has put the revolver back into the pink handbag squeezed tightly beneath her arm. She smells the earth, the soil, the damp roots, she smells the dust, the minerals, the iron and the clay.

Outside it is winter, a bright day, one of those days on which, with its heat and light, the sun tricks us into dreaming about spring, until we reach four in the afternoon.

They don't talk much because they need to conserve their strength to keep moving forward, to keep making progress. They know it's only fifty yards to the exit.

If they make it to the exit.

If the earth doesn't devour them.

A MONTH
BEFORE THE ESCAPE

I

I can't help find it amusing that Daddy is sitting opposite me, in his armchair, drinking whisky from his favourite tumbler, wearing the suit in which we buried him. Outside, the winter sun grants a truce and mothers dash outside, pushing babies in strollers, leading children by the hand. And here I am, shut away at home, talking to a dead man.

How did it happen? Quite simply, one day I heard the key turn in the lock and it was him. It hadn't even been a week, perhaps not even three days, since the funeral.

I know he'll stand up and add another ice cube to his glass to make the whisky go further. I turn away because I don't want to look at him, and instead I watch the sun sinking into the river, tingeing the sky the most beautiful shade of red. He will observe me, he'll clear his throat before he speaks, to gain my attention, and I am already overwhelmed by the thought that he is going to censure my behaviour. What behaviour? Any of it. All of it.

It doesn't matter what I do, it doesn't matter how hard I try to please him, Daddy always finds some defect, something to hold against me. It makes no difference whether I've won a prize for my translation of *Remembrance of Things Past* or if I've just hijacked a truck: in his view, I'll always have done something wrong.

I defend myself before he can attack: I can't let him catch me off guard.

"Yes, Daddy. This morning I stole the cash from a gang of crooks that were hijacking an armoured truck. I showed up, took over the operation, and made off in a van loaded with the loot."

He will return to his armchair and fix me with his gaze; then he'll look at the golden liquid and rattle the ice cubes in his glass. He will sigh. I raise my head and challenge him the way I used to when I was a teenager. I recount details that I know will shock him.

"I shot the Hobo with my .38. I got Diego into the van, and we escaped with the cash. What do you make of that?"

He won't look at me, he'll avoid my eyes. I insist on telling him the most scandalous details until I start to feel ill, until my head hurts, which is what those of us unable to cry do instead of weeping. Then I change tactics, I lower my voice, I appeal for his pity, his compassion.

"I want a different life, Daddy. I want to be a different woman."

He will put down the tumbler before he stands up, before he goes over to the display case full of his Japanese figurines, and I hear the familiar sound of the soles of his shoes creaking on the floor, I see the black leather gleaming. Ever since he died he has recovered the springy step of his younger days. He will stop before the glass-fronted cabinet, he will observe, he will count, one by one, each of the 322 Japanese figures, made of ivory, porcelain, stone, wood; one by one he will inspect the princesses and opera singers and society ladies, the emperors and warriors and monks, the dogs and monkeys and rabbits. He will say they haven't been taken proper care of, that they don't look clean, that they're dusty and I should make better use of the chamois and the flannels he left in the drawer...

I interrupt him.

"I know which drawer you left everything in, and I clean them just like you showed me."

He will shake his head and smile, a smile that says I'm not competent, not efficient, that I don't deserve this legacy.

"No, Daddy, that's not true. I take good care of the figurines. I go over them every Sunday with the brushes and the special cleaning fluids. You can get off my case because I'm not going to listen to you today. The place is exactly as you left it. Every time I open the door and I breathe in its smell, it's as if I'm breathing in the past, the past you left me, as if I'm inhaling every dead member of our family."

In the apartment where I live, there are sighs in dark corners, creaking floorboards, a cold draught blowing across the kitchen worktops. As I walk back and forth, I hear voices, old echoes squeezed in between the walls.

He will return to his armchair, to his whisky. After a few minutes, he'll take out the gold cigarette lighter, perhaps use it to light his pipe. Daddy was a successful man, and he spent his life hoping I would be successful too, that I would embody his idea of a perfect life: an intelligent, slender woman and, at my side, a man like him, cosmopolitan and sophisticated. But I was never slender and I never had at my side a man like the one Daddy would have wanted for me.

The darkness in the room is pierced by little shards of the Montevideo night. I look at him and know he will move on to his next reproach.

"Daddy, don't say that. I don't bite the hand that feeds me. What a horrible expression, 'the hand that feeds you'. How can you say that to me when you used to refuse to feed me, when you punished me by locking me in my room without a scrap of food, so I'd be skinny like Luz and like Mother."

Once again, the memories stir my anger, my resentment; I allow them to flow and multiply, because it's better that way. My rage is the fuel that enables me to keep going. The images flit through my mind, because that's how memories work: they crush us without the least consideration for chronology. I toss more wood on the fire, run through his other criticisms, recall the punishments he inflicted on me, the hunger and the darkness in my bedroom. I don't want this hatred to end because, if it does, guilt will rear its head, and with it will come a pain I know I will be unable to bear. I prefer this buzzing of furious wasps inside my head.

During our lives we gradually grew to hate each other while at the same time we came to resemble each other. Now, ever since his death, ever since I sent him to that mausoleum surrounded by the flowers my sister leaves, we are almost the same person.

For a moment, he will become disturbingly still, his face totally free of expression, and his eyes will look up until his gaze meets my own. A slow smile will sketch itself on his lips.

"No, Daddy. Diego didn't disappear with my share of the money. Give him time, this has only just happened, he's going to call me, you wait and see. He might be a coward but he's a good man, a man of his word. It can't be easy, hiding so much money and struggling with his fear. I know he'll call sooner or later, though, and give me my share of the cash. I trust him. You'll see, Daddy. Sooner or later he'll do the right thing."

And there he sits, silent and motionless, looking at me with his caustic smile until, finally, he raises his arm and takes a long sip of whisky as he ponders what to say next, how to attack me, to wound me. I know what he's going to say.

"I'm not going to renounce the new life that's waiting for me. Ill-gotten gains, you say? Maybe, but I'm not the one who stole it. I took it from the thief and I got away. And you know what? I don't care what you think."

He will look at me suspiciously, preparing his next attack. He'll open his mouth to speak, but I'll beat him to it.

"What do you want to say, Daddy? Well, I don't want to talk any more. Get back to your grave, get back to feeding maggots in that black hole of yours, and don't come out again."

He will shake his head, lower his gaze, feigning sorrow.

"Yes, Daddy, I know I used to listen to you. And I was afraid of you too, even if I didn't show it, even if you thought I was the rebel who defied you, but that defiance was just the form my fear took. I was a wounded animal, lashing out in terror."

I look at him, sitting there, so tall and thin, young and full of vigour despite the fact that he's dead, a steely look in his eyes, his shoes gleaming black, almost ferocious. He will take the golden lighter out again, toying with the flame that appears and disappears. His gaze will turn serious. The gaze that used to make me tremble.

"How much have I suffered because of my fear, Daddy darling? The fear I used to feel. But not any more. Death has tamed your ferocity. You're just one more corpse in the cemetery where your other daughter, Luz, brings you flowers each year. Yes, Luz is lucky – sticking some flowers in a couple of vases is enough to put her conscience at ease. I don't have a conscience, not an easy one or a guilty one, I don't have any debts to settle with the dead, I don't owe them anything I haven't already paid. And I've already collected the debts they owed me. As far as I'm concerned, the dead can rot in hell for all eternity."

There he sits, another reproach forming on his lips, and I feel the fire burning in my guts, my head pounding, and even if it only lasts a second, it's long enough to show that it's not true that time heals everything. Pain endures, it's always there. Why do children inherit a bitter legacy that doesn't belong to them?

The dark doesn't bother me; only the daytime, which is sometimes a slow journey to the night. I move around in the gloom, navigating from memory a house that is always the same. I get up from my chair and walk towards Daddy, I stroke the fabric of his armchair, his empty armchair, the burgundy upholstery, indented where he rested his head against it, the fabric he never wanted to change. Love is a clean, rough diamond; and even if it's too late, now he is dead, I should tell him how much I miss him.

He will walk off into the darkness; I will watch him go and remain silent; I never say anything. Sometimes the dam bursts and I cry, all night long, until dawn breaks.

II

The man wakes up in his bed and opens his eyes like a ventriloquist's dummy. His joints are stiff, his cheeks are pale and sunken, he doesn't dare look around. It's still early. He turns over, lies face up, his eyes like saucers.

The first thought that comes into his mind grabs him by the throat and won't let him go: yesterday was the worst day of his life. For too long, every day has been the worst day of his life.

Sitting up in bed, he grasps his head between his hands, feels a viscous mass between his eyes.

Where did he leave the painkillers? From outside come the muffled sounds of a still-sleeping city, sounds that are amplified by his pain.

He woke up frequently last night, in those moments when time ceased to exist, opening his eyes and longing for it to pass, getting back to sleep only fitfully, interrupted by nightmares.

His second thought, now he is more awake, goes directly to the loot from the hold-up. He thinks about how he left the money in the car, and in his mind an avalanche of questions is unleashed, questions he wanted to avoid yesterday. Will the city still be teeming with cops? What is he going to do with seven bags of cash? Where is he going to hide them? How is he going to shift them from the back seat of the car to a safe place?

He can't avoid the images, the memory of the assault on the armoured truck: a street of grey houses on the outskirts of Montevideo, a neighbourhood of low buildings of brick and unfinished concrete blocks; the white Toyota van and the Nissan, stationary, waiting for the time to come. It's the tense, expectant moment that precedes the attack on the cash truck. Everyone is nervous and impatient, harsh and edgy. Ricardo, alias the Hobo, is in charge. The Hobo curses him, insults him, threatens him; Diego doesn't even remember why. He stays silent, his head down, he's afraid.

The noise of a powerful engine breaks the spell in this street of silent houses. Diego and Ricardo look at each other, their heads turning in perfect synchronicity. The cash truck, early, is approaching from east to west.

The Hobo grunts, the sound you make when you're in the chair, your mouth open and full of cotton wool and metal implements, and the dentist asks you a question. Diego hears him shout: "The truck's coming, it's early. Fuckfuckfuckfuckfuck!"

After that, his memories are fragments: the Hobo running, shots, an explosion, an armoured vehicle in flames. A shout, more shouts, random cries, noises and groans becoming louder. Voices inside the armoured truck. He remembers it well: Ricardo, the Calico in one hand and the .38 in the other, goes straight to the front of the truck. Without opening the door, he unleashes one burst, then another, then a third, although the first is enough to reduce the door to splinters, shear the driver's body in two and blow his companion's face off. There is a dull sound, or at least that's how he recalls it, like an explosion in a feather pillow.

He knows there was another explosion, that he helped the Hobo take the money to the van, but he can't recall anything else about the massacre.

His memory jumps to the moment when the Hobo is standing in front of him, pointing the gun at him, insulting him, about to pull the trigger, to execute him in cold blood; he's afraid, overcome by a wave of nausea, a metallic taste between his teeth. He struggles not to lose consciousness, or maybe he does lose it for an instant, and when he opens his eyes he sees Ricardo, who is no longer pointing the gun at him. Ricardo stumbles, takes a step back. He has a strange expression on his face, his eyes are wide open, he's looking behind Diego. And he falls.

The sky darkens with the speed of an eclipse. Diego follows the direction of Ricardo's gaze and sees Ursula; she is holding a revolver, she puts it in her bag, drinks some water from a bottle. Then she says, "Diego, don't just stand there. Get a move on."

"Ricardo —"

"He's dead – or he will be soon. He was aiming at you, Diego, he wanted to kill you. Didn't you see him? He's a traitor: a traitor and a murderer. I knew him, and I can promise you he wasn't a nice guy."

"Dead?"

"As a dodo, I'd say."

"And you said you knew him?"

"Only in passing. He was the boyfriend of my Auntie Irene's maid."

Then she'll help him into the van with the bags of cash. She'll drive, they'll leave the scene, make their getaway.

Later, somewhere in the city a long way from where the hold-up occurred, they will transfer the cash to Ursula's car, a VW Golf with tinted windows, and each will go their separate way. Ursula will take the van, wipe it clean of prints and dump it, and Diego will keep the VW and the money. They will agree on a rendezvous.

He won't show up. Instead, he'll drive for hours and hours, terrified and sick, gripped by fear; hours during which he will suffer one panic attack after another, an airless infinity, trembling at the thought that the police might catch him and send him back to prison. When he can't take any more, Diego will abandon the car and its contents, parking it on a street a few hundred yards from his apartment, a few hundred yards from the place where he has just woken up.

That was yesterday.

He looks at the green digits on the alarm clock. It's 5.01. His whole body is tingling and his head feels like it's being crushed in a vice.

From the street comes the screech of tyres, the sound of breaking glass, the harsh shouts of a drunk.

He has to get out of bed and deal with the situation. He has to go and get the money. As if he is caught in a nightmare, he thinks, wondering for the first time about the possibility that the money is no longer there, no longer in the car, where he left it covered with a tarpaulin... How long ago was it?

Yesterday, after driving with the cash on the back seat, after swallowing an unspecified number of pills for his anxiety, paralysed and distraught, exhausted and with the fuel tank almost empty, it was all he could do to park the car, lock it and run to his apartment, throw himself into bed and sleep for ten hours straight.

He couldn't think, his head was full of a dull, maddening sound. Had he locked the doors? Had he set the alarm? Ten hours have passed, at least ten. Anything could have happened in that time.

And anyone who robs a thief who has just robbed another thief is surely guaranteed a pardon. He doesn't even want to think about that possibility. His thoughts are enveloped in a kind of fog and have become incoherent: the money must still be there; no, the money isn't in the car any more; yes, the money must still be there. He's going mad. He looks at the clock again and changes position, pulls the covers over his head and immediately pulls them down again. He is in a cold sweat.

The questions return. How can he remove seven bags of money from a vehicle, how can he shift them without being noticed? How can he transport them without help? And where to? How can he find a safe place to keep them? And, above all, how can he avoid the cops who are crawling all over the place?

He's nauseous. He stares into the bottomless pit, on the edge of panic. Where are his anxiety pills? He feels desperate, aware of his cowardice, he feels like crying. The sound of barking, harsh and nearby, disturbs him, makes him sit up, alert.

He thinks: this apartment isn't safe, the police know he lives here. And the lawyer who organized the hold-up, Antinucci, he knows too, and he's bound to come looking for him, to force him to say where the cash is hidden.

Why didn't he think of that earlier?

He has to get up and disappear, take the money somewhere else before daybreak. If there's still time. He tries to concentrate, to put his brain to work.

Getting out of bed, he looks around, his feet planted on the floor. He forces his body to move, gives orders to his legs. He stands up, the palm of one hand pressing against the door frame, the other on his forehead. He moves through the apartment. He has to think of something.

Where are the car keys? He goes from room to room, still drowsy from the sleeping pills. He finds the keys in the bathroom, on top of the pile of clothes he abandoned on the floor.

He looks for the painkillers, pours himself a glass of water, swallows the pills. He turns on the shower.

He stands under the water as it washes away the sweat and the dust, helping to ease his headache.

When he left the vehicle he wasn't thinking about thieves or broken windows or forced locks. He wasn't thinking about the drug addicts, desperate for their next fix, or about the down-and-outs who spend the winter exposed to the elements, huddled beneath the overpasses.

The only thing he was thinking about was evading the police, dodging the roadblocks, hiding from the helicopters in the sky. No, that's a lie. He was also thinking about Ursula and the rendezvous he had missed, thinking about how he had left her waiting in the garage; he was thinking, as he is thinking now, about that strange woman who always seems to be halfway between amusement and rage. In fact, he feels like going to look for her right now.

The water feels cold although it's actually very hot. He shudders and tries to imagine that the shower is summer rain, like the rain that has soaked him so many times before, and he gradually feels better: he closes his eyes, allows the rain to run down his body.

Diego left Ursula's car in an out-of-the-way spot, a place that was the haunt of junkies and homeless people who lived in the doorways of abandoned stores, people who wandered like shadows among ruined houses, who installed themselves in empty buildings or in the cement skeletons of half-built structures.

He gets out of the shower, shaves off two days' worth of stubble, observes the bags under his eyes, the flaccid skin that hangs beneath his chin, the thinning hair on his forehead. Since he returned from Spain, a few months ago, he must have aged ten years. He tries to remember if he has coffee and milk in the house, if there was any bread or butter left yesterday, before he went out to hold up the truck.

Now he needs to find somewhere to hide the cash. He looks out of the window at the same waxy grey sky that has been there for days, the same wet streets. The statue of General Artigas presides over the square, watching the last people returning home and the first setting off for work.

He thinks of something, turns it over in his head.

He looks for the tablet, connects the keyboard, turns it on.

A revelation crosses the threshold of his understanding and lights up his eyes. He looks for a website, reviews options; he has to act quickly, before he is discovered. He has to get out. He finds the option he is looking for, selects it, transfers some money. The ping of his email to confirm the operation fills him with a sense of relief and triumph. It's time to act.

He puts on his coat and prepares to leave.

III

Some people smile because they're friendly, or because they want to look good in a photo or show how white their teeth are. Antinucci, who has had implants to improve the general appearance of his mouth, displays an expression one might almost consider a smile, a peculiar, horizontal grimace, out of sync with the irate tone of his words. A smile that seems, also, to be an expression of anger.

"I'm telling you for the last time. When the armoured truck arrived with the cash, the Hobo was coked up to the eyeballs and Diego was so scared he was like a zombie. Do you understand the situation, Clemen? The Hobo was firing at anything that moved, he left a trail of corpses: all the guards on the truck and even a couple of locals who came out to see what was going on. May they rest in peace."

"Indeed. May they rest in peace."

The bar is a melancholy place, watched over by the glassy eye of a television that shows soccer almost non-stop, as if trying to inject its multicoloured optimism into the grey of the surroundings. Inspector Clemen doesn't know why he always comes to this sad place, perhaps because it is the first establishment to open its doors in the morning. He listens to the lawyer and holds his head in his hands.

"The Hobo and Diego took the money, loaded it into the van, and then this woman appeared."

"A woman?"

"A woman with a gun."

"And who was she? Have you managed to identify her, Antinucci?"

"No, nothing so far. It's a mystery. They'd already loaded up the cash when the woman came over, pointed the gun at the Hobo and fired. I saw it myself, through the telescopic sight. Then she helped Diego into the vehicle and they left."

"But you found her an hour later."

"Yes, I tracked her down because I made sure the vehicle was followed, and I caught up with her while she was trying to get rid of the car. But the cash wasn't there."

"They must have got rid of the bags and she went off to abandon the vehicle."

"I don't know, Clemen, I don't know. When I found the woman and the car there wasn't so much as one stinking peso. But you lot had a GPS on the van. And that means we can reconstruct the route they took and see where they left it."

"I've got the technical report. There are ten minutes when the signal disappeared."

"Why did it disappear?"

"I'll read you the report. 'The majority of GPS failures are due not to the system itself but to the environment in which the transmitter is deployed. For example, if the transmitter is in a basement, if it is subject to jamming – electromagnetic noise which can interfere with the GPS signal – or if it is obstructed by a large concrete structure. There is also the possibility of satellite errors.' That's it. That's all it says."

"Okay, so they entered a multi-storey garage or generated electromagnetic noise or the damn satellite floating around in space failed for precisely the ten minutes when they made the cash disappear. What are you trying to tell me?"

"That they fucked us over."

Meanwhile, on the television, Candidate A is talking, he's wearing jeans and a check shirt, he looks the viewer straight in the eye. He's angry, threatening voters with a return to the bad old days if they don't support him in the upcoming elections.

"Now you've enlightened me with your technical report, Clemen, I'm going to resume my account of yesterday's events."

The inspector listens and wonders if Antinucci always speaks like this. The same grandiloquent phrases, those words nobody understands, certainly not at this time of day.

"As I was telling you, by the time I found the woman she'd dumped the van and didn't have the money bags. I put the squeeze on her, and she told me the cash was with Diego, the patsy, and that both him and the money were in a garage in the Old Town."

"And you believed her."

"I'm going to ignore your irony, inspector. As I was saying: we went to this location, the garage, we went in and – you're never going to believe this – the broad pulled a fast one: she distracted me and escaped through an iron door that led to the neighbouring property. I tried to kick down the door. I went outside, set guards on the place, we surrounded the whole street, eventually we managed to break down the door – it was one of those old ones, the kind that would withstand a grenade – and we searched the

31

property. The place was empty, not a soul. Can you believe that, Clemen? Not a soul."

"She vanished into thin air."

"An escape artist, a new Houdini."

"A new what?"

"How did she do it? I don't know. All we found was a lousy cat. The woman disappeared, she evaporated. Either she escaped over the rooftops, or she turned invisible."

Clemen sighs. On the screen, Candidate B is talking in a sober suit and announcing that he will usher in an instant era of prosperity as soon as the presidential sash is placed over his shoulders. The inspector thinks: Uruguayans have become accustomed to magical realism in politics, even if they don't use the phrase itself. He looks at Antinucci, who seems to be waiting for a solution to the disappearance of the mysterious woman. Clemen doesn't know what to say, so he blurts out the first thing that comes to mind.

"There are lots of tunnels from the colonial period around there."

"You watch too many movies."

"So what happened next, Antinucci? The official version is that all the criminals are dead and all the money was destroyed in the explosion."

Inspector Clemen has just had a cappuccino and two ham and cheese croissants, and his mouth is invaded by stomach acid which tastes of coffee, butter and ham, in that order. He takes a sip of water to get rid of it and gestures to the waitress, who ignores him and walks past. The inspector wonders again why he comes to this bar; the neglect is evident in the grubby crockery and the odour that hits you as you approach the bathroom.

Antinucci's response comes straight away. "I'm going to pay a visit to whoever lives there, next to the garage. String him up, smack him about, kick the shit out of him until he tells me who the hell that woman is."

The second wave of acid arrives.

"For Christ's sake, Antinucci. Let's see if you can get this into your skull – you can't do anything, not right now. Our hands are tied, we have to stay away from this case because there are rumours, rumours that involve you and me."

"What the hell are you talking about? What rumours are these? Why can't I go and look for Diego or for the people who live in the house that the broad used to make her getaway?"

"Listen to me. The word is that we're involved in this armoured truck business."

"The word is, the word is… Whose word?"

"I don't know where the rumours started, I can't be sure. I know Captain Lima has suspected me for a while. What's more, I've heard she has a witness who saw you fire the grenade. If the rumours reach the investigating magistrate, we're both going to get a summons. Do you understand me now?"

The horizontal expression on Antinucci's lips widens a little more, his teeth gleam, white, perfect, new. Clemen glances at the photo of Gardel, looks at the sandwiches on the counter, at the sign on the bathroom door that reads GENTS.

"Let's see if I can unravel it. That bitch Captain Lima thinks she's going to put me in the dock with the evidence of some senile old crow. And that's the only proof she has. She's out of her mind. I'll destroy her, I'll tear her to pieces in front of any court in the land."

"It's not just that. There are people who suspect me too, people who've heard the rumours that you organized the hold-up and I helped arrange it. They've put two and two together, and in a few days they'll be asking for my head. And yours, obviously."

The inspector covers his skull with his hands, with his arms, as if trying to protect himself. Because after the reflux comes the migraine; it's a matter of minutes, as he knows from experience.

Antinucci changes his tone of voice, lowers it to a confidential murmur. "Calm down, Clemen, calm down. I can ask around discreetly, I can send someone to the house where the woman escaped, and to that patsy Diego's place too. I can discreetly —"

The policeman explodes, he gestures impatiently, dejectedly. "We need to keep our heads down! For Christ's sake, Antinucci, the operation to hold up the armoured truck failed. It fucking failed! And the danger is that someone discovers we were behind it. We need to concentrate on saving our asses."

The lawyer's horizontal grimace widens yet further. "You want to carve me out, Clemen. You want to pack me off home, leave me without my share of the loot. Well, I've got news for you: I'm not going to let anyone cut me out. I've invested too much in this business. We embarked on this venture together, and together we're going to find the cash. Or we'll both be taken away in handcuffs."

Clemen feels a shiver run down his spine, and he's not sure if it's the migraine, which has already started, or the lawyer's threat. Before answering, he studies Antinucci's expression, wonders why he finds it so unpleasant, and concludes that, above all, it's because the teeth seem to be a couple of tones whiter than necessary, a couple of sizes larger. He breathes deeply, feels his anger growing, he's not going to allow himself to be scared by some two-bit mafioso with delusions of grandeur. He listens to himself talking, almost shouting. "Antinucci, don't fuck me around, the decision's already been made. You need to disappear for a month. After that, we'll see. I give the orders around here. Is that clear?"

The other man takes a breath, lowers his gaze, appears to be trying to calm himself. He hisses: "I need to find out where the cash is, Clemen. What happened to the money Diego and the woman took? I'm not going to let you tie my hands, not when I'm the one who organized it, the one who made it all happen."

The inspector wipes his hand across his forehead. The difficulties stretch out ahead of him in an interminable line. He reflects that, right now, twenty-four hours after the robbery, he should be enjoying the start of an endless vacation, should be on a beach somewhere, drinking mojitos, swimming in tropical waters. Not here, in this seedy bar across the road from his office, listening to the lies of presidential candidates on the TV and trying to get this prick Antinucci to calm down.

Just then the pain explodes, something shatters inside his head. He asks himself who messed things up. Not him, that's for sure. He kept his side of the bargain, keeping the police away from the scene until the action was over. He kept his side, he thinks again, and he shouldn't have to put up with his strategy being questioned, shouldn't allow the man to reproach him. And yet he hesitates. They're all in the same boat now, and this is no time for arguments and accusations, it's no time to fight when the ship is taking on water. Not yet. He tries to make his partner see reason.

"You've got to understand that the whole thing could get out of control. My job is hanging by a thread. I'm a hair's breadth from getting a phone call from the minister demanding an explanation. And you're two hairs' breadths from getting a summons from the judge. We need to give it some time. We need to put everything on hold. Keep calm, Antinucci, keep calm."

"And what about the money? Are we simply going to let that coward Diego and that woman keep it?"

"Leave it to me. I'll look into what happened with Diego today."

"That's too late. It has to be now, we have to act now."

"My agents are paying a visit to his house this morning. They might already be there. And if he isn't there – and he could be, because the man's a retard – by midday, I'll come up with an excuse for obtaining a search warrant, and we'll tear the place apart, right down to the dirty underwear in the washing machine. The Hobo might also have some information, but he's out of action right now and it's anyone's guess how long for."

Antinucci lowers his voice, leans forward over the table, murmurs into the inspector's ear. "Now you've mentioned the Hobo, I'm going to be blunt: we have to help ferry him across the Styx."

"You what?"

"We have to get him out of the way, rub him out. He's injured, and his prospects are bleak, but if he lives he could be dangerous. He's violent – and he knows far too much about us and the robbery. He's no use to us now anyway. Leave it to me, I'll take care of him."

"We can't. We can't get rid of him. And he might know something, he might have seen something."

Antinucci's teeth appear and disappear between his stiff lips. He spits out his words. "That peasant? He's a piece of shit. He couldn't deal with that woman, the one that shot him and —"

"It always comes back to this mysterious woman."

"I'll catch her, don't you worry."

The lawyer gives a furious laugh, firing droplets of saliva through his teeth like tiny missiles. Clemen decides to have another go at cultivating patience, but with other words. He adopts a conciliatory tone.

"We need to ease off, Antinucci. We can't have any more deaths. Your friend the Hobo has killed enough people already."

Antinucci gulps down the rest of his strong black coffee. "I don't agree. We have to recover the cash and finish off the work we started."

"Right. You want to do away with the Hobo. But who brought him into this in the first place? It wasn't me, it was you."

"Are you criticizing me? What about the police? What did they do? The GPS failed, we lost Diego, we lost the cash. So far, those agents of yours have done nothing to get it back. They haven't lifted a finger, Clemen. Diego, the mystery woman and the cash have all disappeared, vanished into thin air. And what have the police done?"

Clemen thinks this discussion is going on too long. His head is throbbing. Better to shift it down a gear. "Antinucci, this isn't the time for recriminations. We need to find a way out of this situation, and, above all, we need to recover the cash."

"Now we're on the same wavelength. I'm still wondering who started the rumour that we were involved in the hold-up. Are you sure it was the captain? That fucking dyke." The smile on Antinucci's face comes and goes, as if he's suffering from colic.

"I officially forbade her to work on the case, but she had her suspicions and carried on investigating it on her own. I know that yesterday she talked to the old woman, the witness."

"And what did the crone say?"

"I already told you. Apparently the old woman saw you firing a weapon."

"That dried-out fucking hag!"

"Apart from that, I found out that the captain spent all yesterday in a bar on the corner of Treinta y Tres and Sarandí, just opposite the house where that woman disappeared, the one you say has all the money. The one who gave you the slip in the garage. I imagine Captain Lima was hoping she'd show up, or that she's checking out the neighbourhood."

Inspector Clemen shifts in his seat, makes as if to take a sip of his cappuccino from the empty cup. He calls to the waitress again, he wants a Coca-Cola to get rid of the taste of bile. "Leave it to me, Antinucci. I'll deal with it. You go home and keep a low profile for a month, maybe more. Let's see if I can track down Diego and persuade the captain to forget about this case."

"We need to follow the clues: Diego's place and the house next to the garage. You take care of Diego and I'll look for the woman. I'll be discreet, I'll keep a watch on the place, ask the neighbours. If we're stealthy, we won't startle the prey."

He feels the pressure growing as this lawyer stares at him with his eyes like hard-boiled eggs, on his face a bitter smile, the smile of a fake clown. His head feels like it's exploding again. Perhaps the pain or the desire to bring this torture to an end force him to find a glimmer of sense in Antinucci's words. He no longer has the strength to carry on arguing. "Okay, okay. You take care of the woman. And talk to the Hobo. But be discreet about it." Then, for the third time, the inspector calls the waitress, but she ignores him and he gives up.

"Thank Christ, Clemen. I knew you'd come round." As soon as he has said it, Antinucci reproaches himself for taking the Lord's name in vain. Tomorrow he will have to confess, or he will have the shadow of sin on his conscience.

IV

Very early in the morning.

A street in the Old Town, lined by grey buildings, constructions that have managed to survive the influx of money and smoked glass. Crumbling apartment blocks, not yet inhabited by foreign businessmen, windows that open at the start of another day, a day which, like so many others, will be quite uneventful.

A large, dark green door painted many years ago, the street running down to the port, the mist that precedes the rain.

A hesitant hand, a finger that hovers over the names written in pencil. The finger falters, tracks back, finds its target: it reaches out, presses, withdraws and waits.

From the depths of the intercom system, a laboured voice shouts a couple of distorted sentences; it's impossible to know if the voice is that of a man or a woman. The door clicks, and the hand pushes it open and enters the building.

Let us follow. The entrance is dark, gloomy, in keeping with the decrepit floor tiles. The walls are covered with a grey-green stucco fashionable in the 1930s. On the other side of the hall sleeps a birdcage elevator and, next to it, still elegant, sprawls a spiral staircase with worn marble treads.

No doubt the space was once lit by bronze candelabras, their bulbs emitting a soft yellow light, which have been replaced by LED bulbs in metallic fittings, manufactured in some Chinese factory. This harsh light gives the lobby a postmodern appearance – a concept that means anything and its opposite, as we know – like the insides of a spaceship from an old movie.

The floor, also of worn marble, has lost its shine but not its dignity, and the soles of the shoes click across it, performing an involuntary tap dance all the way to the door of the elevator, which scissors open and then closes again with a brisk thump.

This elevator will set off on its journey to the heights, and the harsh light will remain on for another minute. Then the light will go off, but just before it does we will hear one of the doors on the third floor open, only to close a few seconds later.

So let us move to the third floor.

On the door that has just closed are two signs: one which reads DETECTIVE JACK and, below it, another which says ENTER WITHOUT KNOCKING. This seems rather trusting for the times we are in. But the sign is very old, perhaps a few decades, from a time when doors were left open and there was no fear of prowlers sneaking in to see what they could beg, borrow or steal. It is difficult for doors to keep up with the times.

If we enter – without knocking, as the sign instructs – we will find ourselves in a waiting room, a small space that could belong to a lawyer who has not won a case for five years, or a tarot reader whose customers have been seduced by other divinatory arts.

A couple of worn leather armchairs, three posters with fading photos of foreign beaches and a 1980s table which will soon come back into fashion, some gossip magazines. Nothing else.

The owner of the hand is standing in the middle of the room. She seems indecisive or disoriented, as if unsure whether to knock on the glass door or the wooden one, or to wait until she is called and shown through to the other side. The woman is beautiful and thin. Her clothes are finely tailored, she is relaxed, elegant, carrying an expensive-looking handbag. If we consider that clothes are not just a piece of fabric but a message we send to society, then this woman knows exactly what message she wants to send and to whom it should be addressed.

In general terms, she gives the impression that she is not the right kind of client for this establishment because, let's be frank, this woman and whoever owns this office would not appear to be in the same income bracket. She walks over to the door, she appears to be listening or observing, although not much can be seen from this side of the glass, some shadows, one person or two? Through the frosted glass, the light separates out into phantasmagorical images that provide no clarification. A voice, perhaps the same one that answered the intercom a few minutes ago, asks her to wait a second.

There is no answer on this side; the woman turns and walks towards one of the chairs, diverts her gaze to the other chair, finally opts for the first one. Putting the expensive handbag on the table, she opens it, rummages around, takes out a photo and examines it for a few seconds before putting it away. She produces a lipstick and a mirror, proceeds to draw a mouth on her full lips, then looks at her reflection and makes a parody of a kiss for the benefit of the mirror.

The woman sighs, glances at the door. Is she hesitating? Women who visit the offices of private detectives always hesitate.

She looks around, at the table, the chair, the frosted glass door and the wooden one, the posters fixed to the wall with rusty thumbtacks, one that says CALIFORNIA and features a photograph of a wave that must once have been blue yet is now a greenish-yellow, like stagnant pond water, and a blonde surfer who must now be old and grey. The other is of a beach with palm trees; it doesn't give the location, but it's no doubt somewhere in the Caribbean, and if we think about it, it's possible that today that white sand is covered with old tyres and plastic bags or has been concreted over to build a resort.

The woman stares down at the table; there is an even layer of dust, disturbed only by the silhouette left by her bag and a circle marking the exact spot where somebody put down a glass. There's not much more to see, and the inspection comes to an end at this point.

She appears to be unimpressed; she purses her lips in an expression that could denote displeasure, concern or impatience. To judge by her wrinkled nose, she doesn't like the smell floating in the air, and we can agree that she's not entirely wrong, because the air is heavy with cigarette smoke despite the prohibition on smoking in public premises. It's shocking the way some people have no respect.

The woman discovers some more magazines on a shelf underneath the table. She picks them up, looks at them, leafs through the first one. *True Crime*, the magazine is called. She smiles at the title: what a cliché. The others are more issues of the same publication.

"Come in, please," says a voice on the other side of the door, in the office.

The woman looks up, shakes the magazines, tosses them down next to her on the chair. She stands, picks up her bag (which, now we are closer, we can confirm is a very expensive brand), advances towards the frosted glass door, pushes it open. She enters. Unfortunately, there is nothing of interest to describe in this office, just a battered old oak desk, three drawers on one side, three on the other (one of the drawers, the third on the left, refuses to open), four yellow diplomas, chairs that have nothing in common either with each other or with the desk, a window in a rusty iron frame which looks onto the street and leaks a little when the wind blows the rain from the west.

The woman stands in the doorway, facing the person at the desk. Her mouth appears tense, the corners turned slightly downwards. Her right hand clutches the bag, the bag presses against her ribs. An insect flits in front of the light and a distorted shadow is projected onto the wall, something that does not resemble a fly but rather a moving filament.

V

There is an old apartment, decrepit, a kitchen bathed in early-morning sunlight, a table and a chair, a woman, her body taut, her face tense, her forehead wrinkled: the woman is eating soup; on the table is a check cloth which looks vintage.

In the apartment it smells musty, of yellowing photos and worm-eaten books. The rugs are threadbare. And the kitchen tablecloth is simply old.

The woman isn't even watching the television or listening to the radio, as she usually does, she hasn't read a book or made a start on the translation assignments piling up on the table. She doesn't look out at the estuary: she eats, and waits for a phone call. And she thinks.

She contemplates her life through the steam rising from her soup. Her wrist, the strap of her watch squeezing the flesh, moves nervously from the spoon to the napkin and from the porcelain bowl to the glass of water. Hers is a life of silent telephones and boiled pumpkin, a life lived beneath a fine layer of dust. She swallows the soup, knowing it will never satisfy her hunger. Hers is a life of silences interrupted only by the noises of others, by prolonged silences displaced as the evening wears on by the sound of televisions, of footsteps, of voices. The woman at the table, the one waiting for a call as she drinks her soup, the one thinking about her house and her life, is Ursula.

I am Ursula.

I am the woman waiting for a phone call, a life change, a new image, the woman waiting for the opportunity to emerge from this carapace of obesity. Crouching here, I wait for the chance to become someone else.

I told Daddy last night, but he doesn't listen to me, he just wants to criticize me for every act and omission I perpetrate. That's the verb he uses when he talks about what I do: *perpetrate*. I've never asked him why.

It wasn't easy for me to tell him I'd met a man who'd invited me to take part in holding up an armoured truck; it sounded too grandiose to tell him that I arrived at the scene of the attack when everything was in chaos, that I shot the Hobo, that I bundled Diego into the van and fled with him and the stolen money. Put like that, it sounds artificial, made up, like something from a cheap action movie.

The best part of the story is that it worked out; we pulled off the heist and managed to escape before the police arrived. We fled and then we split up. I dumped the van, Diego left in my VW with the cash, and we were going to meet up later at a safe location: the garage I rent from the bookstore, where I keep my car. That part didn't work out so well, and Diego disappeared.

He disappeared with the money. With my money.

Don't be so dramatic, Ursula, don't lose hope: he's going to call.

Meanwhile, I can't afford to sit doing nothing and I mustn't lose my cool; I have to be careful, take the necessary precautions, get rid of any trace there might be of yesterday's actions. I have to concentrate on that, on eliminating the evidence.

Go through your checklist, Ursula.

The revolver I used to shoot the Hobo with has already been meticulously cleaned with solvent, the bothersome and persistent particles left by the explosion have been removed, the weapon has been sealed in an impermeable bag and placed in an old, disused drainpipe, which I then covered with cement and its corresponding floor tile.

Check.

I had to read up on firearms and, above all, on what happens when you discharge them, although that was the least of it, because the internet is full of maniacs who seem to love shooting their friends and family.

And it turns out that firearms produce something called gunshot residue, caused by the deflagration of powder which issues from the revolver barrel, or so I read on criminalistic.com. This residue is usually deposited on hands and clothes. Barium, antimony and lead form a cloud that is emitted at high speed and adheres to nearby objects: for example, the hands, face and clothes.

For my own clothes, which presumably bore traces of powder, I followed the advice of killersunited.tv: I cut them into strips and disposed of them in a dozen different garbage containers which, if everything goes smoothly, will be collected tonight and be at the dump by dawn, where they will be lost and contaminated until the end of time.

Check.

Scientific procedures such as the paraffin test can be used to detect gunshot residue and identify who pulled the trigger, according to murderersonline.org, who suggest three ways of removing traces, none of which is completely reliable, they warn.

It will be far from easy to get rid of the traces that no doubt cling to my hands. According to my understanding, there are lots of recipes for getting rid of them, from urine to turpentine, but the experts explain that it's all for nothing if the police apply the relevant expertise. Something which seems unlikely to happen here in Uruguay. However, I like to imagine there is a brilliant mind on my trail, supported by cutting-edge technical resources – the sodium rhodizonate test, for example – and I do everything within my power to outwit them, as if I was dealing with the kids from *Quantico*.

But getting back to what we were saying: if nothing can remove gunshot residue, why am I complicating matters with these hard-to-find corrosive products that will only ruin my hands? I will follow the advice of murderersonline.org.

It won't be difficult; tonight is San Juan, the longest night of the year down here in the southern hemisphere, the winter solstice, and there are festivities in the squares of the Old Town. Festivities with fireworks. Fireworks with gunpowder. Gunpowder on the hands and arms and faces of everyone there.

I'll go down to buy some firecrackers and some rockets, and let them off surrounded by people from the neighbourhood who have known me all my life, people who one day can swear they saw me setting off fireworks.

Tonight I will think about the residue on my skin, the residue from the shot, which will be masked by the gunpowder from the celebrations.

Check.

VI

Diego has just collected the keys to a new apartment from the supervisor's office; they are jangling in his pocket and he looks pleased with himself. He won't go back to his old place: he's rented another one in the same building, via a temporary accommodation website.

Fictitious name, fake email, payment by anonymous transfer, all via the Dark Web and the Tor browser so his IP address remains hidden.

Why in the same building? He knows that in a few hours the police or Antinucci's people will turn his place upside down. And he wants to be nearby, to guard the guards, so to speak and, above all, to know as soon as possible when the coast is clear again. He doesn't want to endanger Ursula: he'll call her as soon as the danger is past.

In the old place he left everything as it was – the bread from his breakfast the day before, the cups with dried-out stains, the unmade bed – and took a last look around, aware that he wouldn't be able to return for a long time, that he might never return. All he took was the blue suitcase, the one he brought with him from Spain, then he locked the door carefully, the top bolt and the two lower ones. If they want to get in, they'll have to work for it.

He catches the elevator, crosses the lobby, leaves the Palacio Salvo dragging the suitcase behind him. It's still dark.

We shouldn't be misled by the name: the Palacio Salvo is not a palace but a huge apartment block that was once the glory of Montevideo, the tallest building in South America. That was many years ago, though, and now it is a ramshackle shadow of its former self. If buildings had souls, we could say Salvo is striving to maintain its art deco dignity despite the plastic fittings and cheap tiles that have replaced the metalwork and the marble, despite the man who sells Chinese watches from a folding table at the door, despite the supervisor, who has just given Diego the keys and now sits on the other side of a chipboard counter, staring at the screen of his computer.

Diego goes out through the main door, into the arcade that smells of piss, turns left, then right. The vast space of Plaza Independencia and the proximity of the estuary combine to create a different hurricane at each corner. He turns again, and the wind hits him in the face, lifts the empty suitcase, causes the overcoat to billow around his thin body. His step becomes more uncertain as he approaches the place where he thinks he left the car; he stops, hesitates. Was it here or further on? This block or the next one? Perhaps further east? He continues, tries to concentrate, to remember what happened last night; his gaze slides across the storefronts, he strives to focus on the window displays. Anxiety takes hold, the same fear as always, and he starts to sweat. He forces himself on, he drags his suitcase, kicks a plastic bottle out of the way, is assailed by a plastic bag. He swallows bitter saliva.

The two blocks at the western end of Calle San José are a frontier with the underworld, one that appears to be populated by zombies escaped from a third-rate horror movie. He makes his way through down-and-outs cooking on the sidewalk, addicts dressed in rags, women carrying babies and pleading for a few coins to buy milk.

Diego looks away from this scene of misery, into the distance. He thinks he's spotted the VW Golf, about a hundred yards away. Is that it? A man appears from behind a garbage container and they almost crash into one another. A little further on, he dodges a shadow lying prone on the ground, jumps over two legs that end in bandaged feet. The vision is disturbing, hair-raising, and it reminds him of jail, of the horror and violence of prison.

This thought sets off an alarm and puts him on guard: when he thinks about prison, everything else becomes hazy and blurred. He needs to push away these images and escape.

He takes out a pill, swallows it, squeezing his lips until they hurt, feels his stomach tighten, does up his overcoat, quickens his pace, sidesteps a dog that growls at him.

Yes, that's the one, Ursula's VW Golf; he has it in his sights, he fingers the keys in his pocket.

A gust of wind pushes him in the opposite direction, lifts the suitcase from the ground; he bows his head and attacks, setting himself against the forces of nature. He glances over his shoulder: fierce expressions, menacing hands thrust into deep pockets, threatening mouths, open and toothless. He has the impression that someone is following him. He wipes his forehead with the back of his hand. He speeds up, trying to leave behind the shadow that appears to be following him; he overtakes a woman who, her head also bowed, turns around and looks at him with strange eyes, looks at him and at the blue suitcase.

He needs to calm down. The car is there, a few yards away, none of the windows appear to be broken and, thinking about it, who would imagine this old piece of junk contains a small fortune?

Diego must overcome his fear and act normally. He calms down, or at least he thinks he does.

He finally reaches the car, checking once again that the key is still there, in his pocket. The shadow approaches and he hears a voice, whispering behind him, over his right shoulder. Fetid breath invades his space, the man asks him for some money in a hollow murmur. Diego turns and they face each other, the man's nose a few inches from his own, he hears the breathing, sees the dilated pores, the yellow teeth. He looks away and rummages in his pockets, looking – or pretending to look – for the coins the man is asking for. Diego places the suitcase between them, as if building a barrier. He finds a banknote and takes it out, afraid it will be too much, that the man will realize he is willing to pay whatever it takes to get rid of him. But no, he holds the note out, just twenty pesos, an insult almost, and what he feels is not fear but shame. He mutters an apology and hands over the note. The man takes it without saying thanks, all the time looking him straight in the eyes, not retreating an inch.

Diego perspires, fights the urge to run, to abandon everything. He inhales deeply, faces the man, inspects the mouth that opens and speaks, smells the breath that stinks of rotten teeth, of cheap wine, of indigestion. The mouth whispers words Diego doesn't catch. He asks the man to get out of the way, tries to push him with the suitcase, attempts to dislodge him, to gain enough space to move, to turn around and get in the car.

Another man, perhaps one of the group that was sitting around a fire, has approached unnoticed and now stands next to the one who is whispering at him, so Diego is boxed in against the car. Now there are two faces, two noses with their dilated pores, two mouths, and now they are not whispering: they are demanding. Louder and louder.

The two faces are very close; the mouths open and spit out the stench of sour wine, of poverty. Their voices grow louder still; they are shouting. He is penned in, he knows he should turn around and open the door, put the suitcase in the vehicle, get in and leave as quickly as possible. Or follow his instincts and abandon it again, run home, climb into bed. He wipes the sweat from his forehead.

He feels for the pills but can't find them.

The dogs bark. Every dog in the city barks.

He thinks he hears a police siren. He looks to the corner and spots a patrol car approaching from the Old Town. It is moving at walking pace, and Diego immediately understands who they are looking for. He has to hide, get away.

Following his gaze, the two men turn their heads towards the west, see the patrol car. They look at each other, the corners of their mouths curving forward and upward, in a signal. Diego watches them hesitate then retreat. They are no longer paying attention to him, no longer shouting. They are whispering, talking to each other in low, urgent voices, they turn and move away. As they go, he sees them looking over their shoulders, sees the fleeting fear in their faces, sees them run.

The patrol car also detects the sudden movement and heads towards them, accelerating with a strident screech of its tyres. Diego crouches down and hides behind the Golf. The police pass by without seeing him, the car turns sharply north, it disappears. He hurries up, manages to insert the key in the lock despite his trembling hands, manoeuvres the suitcase onto the front passenger seat, walks around the car and gets into the vehicle on the driver's side.

He sits there, his neck rigid, not daring to look behind him, afraid he will turn his head and see that the money is no longer where he left it the night before.

Diego lowers the window a little, fills his lungs with the salty air blowing in from the estuary, leans his forehead on the steering wheel and rests for a few seconds. He feels drops of sweat sliding down his face, dripping from his nose onto his coat. Finally, he turns his head, looks at the back seat and lifts the tarpaulin. All the bags are there, thank God, all the money is there.

Now he must leave without wasting any time. He starts the engine and puts the car into first gear; as he does so, he sees the first light of the morning sparkling in the puddles on the tarmac and – who knows why? – feels it is a good omen. He heads south, sees the sun above the horizon.

He looks at the money again in the rear-view mirror: the sight has a calming effect. The fear begins to disperse, the desire to flee slowly dissipates.

He will let some time pass, wait until they stop watching his house; when everything is calm he'll call Ursula and deliver her share of the loot, give back this car. Yes, he'll let a few days pass. It'll be good for him to rest, to calm down, to wait in his new place until the police get bored of searching for him.

For the first time in hours he manages to fill his lungs with air, he is no longer shaking, his senses start to clear. He sees a flock of sparrows in a tree's bare branches, a reddish gleam tinges the sky and the clouds, he finds the bland landscape of the estuary a relief.

The car disappears in the direction of the coast.

VII

"Come in, please."

The woman stops at the door, hesitates. "I was looking for Jack."

"I'm Jack."

"But you're a woman." Any feminist organization on the planet would have condemned her tone. And she regrets the words as soon as they leave her mouth. She hurries to make amends. "It doesn't matter, of course."

"Jacqueline Daguerre, pleased to meet you. You can call me Jack. Have a seat."

"I thought…"

We will never know what she thought, because the sentence is left floating in the air, like a wisp of doubt that arrived and then left.

"Yes, lots of people think."

Jacqueline – we will use the full version of her name, at least for now – says this in a whisper, as if talking to herself. She isn't upset or offended, just a little tired of fighting against certain prejudices that don't do her business any good, the stereotypes so prevalent in the private investigation sphere.

There are days she wishes she was a heavily built man in a raincoat, and not this slight, almost insignificant woman.

———

With a gesture, she invites her visitor to come in and sit down. Jack knows what the woman will say next, she's heard it so many times. She closes her eyes and listens.

"People told me about this agency, but I thought the director was a man."

"My grandfather was the first Detective Jack; the second one was my father – I learned the trade from him. I draw on three generations of experience in this job."

"And where's your father now?"

Jacqueline knows there's no way out of this one: reluctant as she is, she has to lie, but only a little, it's almost a white lie. "He's on a trip."

We should clarify that Mr Daguerre is indeed on a trip, although she has omitted to mention that he has gone on the trip that awaits us all, one from which there is no return.

"Tell me about the case." Jacqueline prefers to get to the point without being distracted by such details.

The woman's hand, which has been clutching the bag all this time, finally grants itself a respite, loosens its grasp on the straps, falls to her lap and rests there, the fingers outstretched. She runs her hand over her hair, smooths it down a bit. She looks at Jacqueline and tries to decide how much to tell her. "There's somebody I want you to investigate."

"Your husband? Did he disappear? Has he left you? Is he cheating on you?"

"No, nothing like that. Why would you assume I'm looking for my husband or that he must be cheating on me?"

"I'm sorry, force of habit."

"Well, I'm not here because of my husband. I decided to hire a detective to investigate somebody, she's called Ursula López and…" The woman's hand tenses again, the thumb disappears into the palm, the hand forms a fist, she looks at the shadow of the fly that has neither wings nor legs and doesn't even look like an insect, just a strange, elongated form that could be a worm. "I have… some suspicions."

"What kind of suspicions?"

The woman pauses, gathers herself. "Before I continue, I want to clarify something. I'm Ursula's sister. My name is Luz López."

Detective Jack shows no surprise, her expression does not change; if we observe her carefully, we will notice she is concealing a yawn, the effect perhaps of digestion or simply of the stuffy air.

Right now she is neither happy nor unhappy, merely a little bored. She picks up a card; it looks like one of those index cards people once used, before the arrival of computers, to record the names and addresses of clients, recipes, the phone numbers of locksmiths. One of those old-fashioned filing cards, we might say, a rectangular relic from the pre-computer Palaeolithic. We wonder if this resistance to change is a defining feature of Jacqueline Daguerre's personality, and, as we don't have the answer, all we can do is pay attention. Let us continue.

"I'm going to ask you for some information before we get into the subject. How did you say you'd found out about me? Did somebody recommend me?"

"I was at a meeting and somebody mentioned the agency and gave me your address, I don't remember who. I didn't call first because all I had was an address and I couldn't remember who had given it to me."

"How strange that they gave you my address but didn't tell you I was a woman." Jack can't help sounding annoyed, and there is an awkward moment.

"I guess it must seem strange. But my memory…" Luz gestures vaguely, alluding to her forgetfulness, to indicate that the explanation is over, then dictates her name and phone number.

There is a silence.

"My situation is delicate, I have to be sure of the utmost confidentiality."

"Of course. Everything we discuss will be strictly private."

"It's a complicated affair. It started with a murder. Of my Auntie Irene."

"I can assure you that in such cases our confidentiality is absolute."

The woman sitting across from the detective hesitates, directs her gaze through the window, at the letters reading BAR. Jack observes her and thinks she is very beautiful, something of which she is surely aware; however, she also appears to have decided not to make this information public, reserving it instead for herself or for the time and the person she chooses. Elegant and beautiful, Jack thinks, attractive without being showy, seductive but understated. She listens to her speak.

"It's not easy to say, but I have my suspicions."

"Tell me about the murder of your Auntie Irene."

Luz López sighs, looks to one side and then the other. It all began as an innocent intellectual game, motivated by a couple of possibly groundless suspicions, an unlikely jigsaw puzzle, an exercise in dispelling doubt. She makes up her mind, crosses the Rubicon and starts to tell the story.

"My Auntie Irene was murdered more than a year ago. The police found the killer immediately, he was the boyfriend of my Auntie Irene's maid. They found the murder weapon with his prints on it. He was called Ricardo, but he went by the nickname of the Hobo. He'd taken a lot of drugs. The investigation found he had killed her to steal a very valuable ring, a piece of jewellery which disappeared that day and was never found again. That's one part of the story, a part I thought was closed."

"So there's a second part?"

"Yes. There's another part that's connected to this story."

Jacqueline observes the woman's unblinking eyes, her pale knuckles gripping the straps of the bag, the mouth that moves just enough to emit the gentle sound of her voice, and she doesn't know what to think of what she's heard. And so she doesn't think anything. She waits. The woman continues.

"Just over a month ago my boyfriend, Santiago, was kidnapped."

"Are you single?"

"It's complicated. I'm in the process of divorcing my first husband."

"Of course. Carry on, please."

"Santiago was kidnapped, I was saying. They held him captive in an abandoned farmhouse. But his kidnapper fell asleep, my boyfriend managed to get his phone, he located the place with the GPS and notified the police. And he also notified me."

"Sounds like the kidnapper was something of a novice."

Luz appears not to be in the mood for jokes, and she continues with her account. "Santiago sent me the coordinates, otherwise there's no way I would have been able to find it. Camino del Quebrado is the name of the road. Have you ever heard of it?"

"I'm afraid not. And did they release your boyfriend?"

"Yes, it all turned out fine. The police got there before me, and they arrested the kidnapper. He'd taken sleeping pills and was out cold. Can you believe it?"

"The criminal sounds like a bungling idiot."

"And now I'm getting to the interesting part. Before I reached the hiding place, the shack where Santiago was being held, the GPS stopped working and I lost my way. Confused, I got out of my car, and saw a vehicle approaching. Some important details: it was night-time, I was in the middle of nowhere, and it was raining. I stopped the other car, which looked familiar, and who do you think was driving it? My sister, Ursula. In the middle of nowhere, on a dark, rainy night."

"What was she doing there?"

"That's what I asked her. She gave me an explanation that was logical but improbable: she'd been to a dinner party at a friend's farmhouse, she was on her way home and, like me, had got lost."

"It doesn't sound all that improbable."

"If you knew Ursula you'd know she doesn't have any friends, she doesn't go to dinner parties, and she hardly ever goes out at night."

"Don't take offence, but I don't think that's sufficient reason to rule it out."

"You're right. But there's more." She shakes her head, closes her eyes, as if trying to clarify her thoughts or to say something difficult. Suddenly she seems tired. "When she opened the window and I saw it was her, the first thing that surprised me was that she was wearing gloves."

"That's not so strange. Plenty of people wear gloves when they drive. Particularly in winter."

"They were latex gloves, Jack. I asked her why she was wearing them."

"Latex? I guess that is a bit odd. And what did she say?"

"She pulled them off, threw them away, and didn't answer me. I was staring at her fingers. And what do you think she had on her right hand? Auntie Irene's ring."

"The one supposedly stolen by the murderer?"

"The very same. Well, obviously I asked her where she'd got it from. She told me she'd found it that afternoon, while she was sorting out some boxes of things that had belonged to our aunt."

"Something makes me think you didn't believe her. Am I right?"

"My aunt always wore that ring. And when she took it off, she put it in the safe, because it was valuable. So it's unlikely it would have been jumbled up with letters and souvenirs." Luz leans back in her chair and takes a deep breath before continuing. "I've suspected for some time that my sister hadn't told me the whole truth about what happened that afternoon, when my aunt was murdered. And I don't think she's told me everything she knows about my father's death, either."

"What were the circumstances of your father's death?"

"He died of an overdose of Somnium."

"Is that a brand of sleeping pills?"

"Yes."

"Do you think it was suicide?"

"That's what Ursula thinks. And that was the coroner's verdict."

The woman is silent, the account appears to be over.

She seems a little older than when she came through that door, fifteen or twenty minutes ago.

"Why haven't you told the police about this?"

"I don't want to drag the police into this. She's my sister. Do you understand? These are family affairs."

"So what exactly do you want me to investigate, Luz?"

"Everything to do with my sister. I want to understand her. What she does during the day, if she goes out at night, where she goes, who she meets."

"So tell me what it is you suspect."

"I don't know what I suspect. I don't have any evidence of anything, just scraps of conversations, the odd observation, looks and glances."

"Luz, I'm not even sure if I'm going to accept this case, but you have to help me, and you have to tell me the truth. All of it."

"I think Ursula is hiding something about the deaths of Daddy and Auntie Irene. That she knows more than she lets on. That there's a link between the two deaths."

"Okay. Do you have a photo of your sister?"

"Here you are."

Luz takes out a photo and places it on the desk. The detective picks it up. "An attractive woman."

"Ursula is very pretty."

Jacqueline could take notes to keep her left hand busy – did we mention she is left-handed? – but she thinks it would be pointless to write down information that may well be useless in the near future. Because no detective agency that investigates unpaid debts, thefts between neighbours, and unfaithful spouses would ever accept this case: the whole affair smells fishy from a mile away. Not to mention that she is about to go off on vacation, she has reserved a room in a little hotel, on a quiet beach, out of season.

But how does one decide such things?

What pushes us to accept a role in a story? Jack accepts – who knows why? – and now she is taking notes and writing down addresses and phone numbers. She'll start right away.

VIII

Here comes Antinucci, with neither an umbrella nor a coat, the rain pouring down mercilessly. Observe the expression on his face: his bulging eyes, his flared nostrils, the corners of his mouth rigid and horizontal, as if a smile had been embedded in his face. He has a grimace of annoyance that promises no good.

The scar above his right eyebrow looks like it was made by a fist, or perhaps he fell off his bike when he was a kid, who knows? He walks very upright, with a martial step, his arms swinging, the document case held slightly away from his body, and in his head "The Ride of the Valkyries" plays. He jumps to avoid the water gushing from the drains.

The rain performs a choreography around him, as if he is surrounded by gyrating ghosts.

And then, from one moment to the next, the rain will stop, leaving a fog that blurs the outlines of the city.

Before he enters the hospital Antinucci shelters under the porch, lights a cigarette and smokes it all the way down until all that remains between his lips is a tiny stub, which he takes between his fingers and flicks into the angle formed by the asphalt and the kerb. He has to stop smoking, he's been telling himself for years, he knows he must give up this disgusting habit, and he hates himself for his inability to do so. He's made up his mind, he's going to sign up for the Quit Smoking programme. As soon as he's dealt with the Hobo, he's going to make an appointment. Today, right now.

Water pours from the statues adorning the hospital facade, water that has fallen from the sky like tears, like spit, like piss, spattering the passers-by with pent-up hatred, splashing our lawyer's Italian moccasins.

Antinucci takes out two antacid pills, pops them into his mouth and hurries into the lobby. He looks at his shoes, the shine ruined, and tries to shake the water from the sleeves of his blue suit jacket. He manages to hold back a curse he was on the verge of uttering, blocking it before it can besmirch the state of sanctity he enjoys of a morning, that state of purity which comes from attending Mass and confessing. Let us delay our explanation of this defining aspect of our lawyer no longer: he is a pious man with a deeply held faith, a man who enjoys the smell of wax and incense, who delights in and is moved by the prayers of Father Ismael at the church of Las Esclavas del Sagrado Corazón on Calle Ellauri.

He swallows the pills, stops in front of the reception desk, and asks. He gives the name of the patient; the receptionist consults her screen and gives him a number: 522. The woman explains where he needs to go, points it out to him, and he feels as if he is about to enter a labyrinth: he has to go down three corridors, turn right, go through two more doors and then turn left, take the Block B elevator to the fifth floor, turn left again and continue to the end... Before he reaches Block B he's already forgotten the instructions and he stops, annoyed, confused, asks again, listens to another explanation of a route impossible to follow without a theodolite and a sextant. Again he feels the urge to curse, again he bites his tongue. After wandering around for a while, half by chance, he finds himself standing in front of room 522.

Next to the door is a chair, in the chair is a policeman, in the policeman's hand is a telephone. Antinucci observes him frantically tapping away, and assumes there must be a game on the phone screen, with racing cars, soldiers killing one another or monsters being trapped and devoured.

The lawyer knows what to do.

He allows his shadow to fall on the chair next to the door to room 522, onto the policeman who is on guard, onto the screen of the phone. The agent takes a few seconds to look up.

"Good morning, officer."

"Good morning."

"I'm Mr Antinucci. I represent Ricardo Prieto, the patient in this room. I have permission to talk to my client, who was admitted yesterday morning and is in a serious condition." Antinucci's voice is hard, dry, clipped. His appearance matches his voice and, despite the rainwater still dripping from his clothes, his dignity is almost untouched. The policeman stands up, the phone in his right hand. He looks at Antinucci, looks at the screen, looks at Antinucci again.

"The prisoner is in a coma. He's in isolation. You're going to need authorization from a magistrate and…" The policeman positions himself between Antinucci and the door.

"I know he's in a coma. And I already have authorization. I want to go in and see my client, confirm his condition.

Have you been here all morning? You should have received a notification from Criminal Court Number 5. I'm assuming you received it first thing."

"Well… no, I'm not sure, to be honest. I don't think it's arrived yet…"

"The usual inefficiency. Please call them to check. I don't have all day. I'm assuming you have the number for Criminal Court Number 5." The lawyer's face is like a mask carved in stone.

"Hang on… I'm not sure I've got the number and…"

Antinucci checks his wristwatch, an object we hope to come back to, if we have time. But not right now, when we find ourselves in the middle of a tussle, although we know in advance that the lawyer will win effortlessly. Let us continue with the scene.

"Officer, I only have a few minutes. The judge told me personally that —"

"That man won't be able to tell you anything just now. Even if he wanted to. Like I said, he's in a coma."

"I know that, officer. I need to confirm his condition personally. I would be grateful if you could do as I asked and phone the court."

The policeman looks at him, looks at the screen of the phone as if it might contain a miraculous solution – or the number the lawyer is asking him for – then looks at Antinucci again.

"All right. You can go in, sir."

"Thank you."

"Just be aware of the patient's condition."

"I understand, officer."

Antinucci makes a small gesture with his hand, brief and powerful, with sufficient energy to shift the policeman to one side, clearing his passage to the room. The gesture has no importance for the scene we will shortly witness. However, we highlight it because it gives a full-length portrait of the lawyer: one man displaces another, larger man with the slightest gesture of his hand.

He enters and closes the door behind him. He turns and faces the bed.

There lies Ricardo Prieto, alias the Hobo, a heavyweight criminal both inside and outside prison.

We know he is in a coma, although at first sight he gives the impression that he is asleep. We might even say he is pretending to sleep. His eyes are closed. If he were to open them, we would see that they are red, as if in a bad photograph; red eyes that bore into people, eyes that induce a shudder in anyone they rest upon.

The Hobo's skin is tattooed with skulls, their eye sockets glowing. Gothic letters form names, painted blood gushes across his body. The tattoos peer out above his standard-issue sky-blue hospital pyjamas; they extend along his arms and his legs, ascend his chest, clamber up his neck to his face: an impressive demonstration of blood-curdling body art. His fingers are as thick as branches, they are forceful fingers with strong opinions, fingers that are not afraid to squeeze. His pyjama top is open and over his stomach is a broad, white bandage, thick at the navel.

Antinucci, a man not given to doubt and hesitation, approaches and sits next to the patient, on the bed. He rests a hand on either side of the man, leans over, brings his head close to the Hobo's face. He speaks in a low tone, stressing the opening words and the patient's name.

"Wakey-wakey. Your sick leave is over, Hobo."

The man doesn't open his eyes or move a single muscle; from his chest comes the harsh, hollow sound of angry breathing, laboured panting.

The lawyer waits, his face close to the Hobo's. A horizontal line forms on his lips, as if he were about to smile. But he doesn't smile and he doesn't say anything. His expression turns to one of irritation.

He stands up next to the bed, crosses his arms, his head slightly inclined to one side. He allows a minute to pass, two, the only sound the noise of Ricardo's breathing, mixed with the pitter-patter of rain against the window. Antinucci feels the moisture on his clothes gradually transform into steam under the influence of the hospital's heating system. He checks his watch again, this time impatiently.

"Hobo."

Ricardo remains mute, motionless.

"Listen to me. Listen very carefully."

Antinucci sits back down on the bed, once again positioning one arm at either side of Ricardo. He speaks in whispers, his mouth almost touching the other man's ear.

"It all went wrong, Hobo. It all went to hell, and now Inspector Clemen wants heads to roll. Yours first, obviously. And mine. So I need to try and find out what happened. Let's start at the beginning. Before that woman turned up and shot you, what happened exactly?" Silence. The Hobo remains stubbornly immobile. "I'm going to help you, Hobo. The cash truck took a direct hit from a projectile fired by yours truly, and the vehicle went up in flames. Do you remember? So far, so good." The man in the bed doesn't open his eyes, doesn't move his lips. "The truck exploded. And, with Diego's help, you loaded the bags of cash into the van. What happened next? You pointed your gun at Diego, I saw you through the telescopic sights. And who the hell was that woman, the one who appeared out of nowhere and shot you? She escaped with Diego and with the cash. I had her followed, I caught up with her, and she suggested we split the loot. What a nerve! But she tricked me. She took me to a garage and told me Diego would show up with the money. And, somehow, she managed to slip out of my grasp. I won't even tell you what happened, it would only upset you. So, who was the woman that shot you and made off with my money, Ricardo?"

Nothing.

Antinucci is still hunched over the bed, and his head, neck and shoulders are starting to ache. He wipes his forehead, runs his hand over his wet hair, rubs his eyes. The door bangs loudly against the wall; a woman in a white lab coat bursts in and, from the arrogant, scornful expression on her face, it would be impossible to confuse her with anyone who is below God. In other words, she's a doctor.

"You have to leave immediately."

"I've been granted authorization —"

"I'm going to call Security if you don't leave right now, sir."

"My name is Antinucci."

The doctor appears unimpressed. "The patient is in a coma and is in no condition to receive visitors. I'm asking you to leave."

"I'm going, doctor. I just wanted to check my client's condition in person. I'll be back. Have a good day."

Antinucci takes out two more antacid tablets, swallows them. He starts to reach for the packet of cigarettes and immediately remembers his good intentions. He's going to make an appointment with Quit Smoking or whatever they're called. His fingers make contact with the pack again. He takes it, puts a cigarette in his mouth.

IX

The car rattles over the wet, uneven surface. After driving for a few minutes, Diego will stop the car in a quiet side street near the shore. He will look at the horizon, enveloped in black storm clouds, and – like every inhabitant of Montevideo – he will ponder the mercurial climate in this city of winds.

In the rear-view mirror he will glance at the bulky form that lies on the back seat, somewhat askew after the journey, and he will look at the blue suitcase on the seat next to him. The view provides an injection of enthusiasm. He will feel his hands tremble, his teeth chatter. He knows it isn't going to be easy to remove the contents of the bags, transfer them to the suitcase, count the money under the nose of whoever happens to be passing by. But in his favour are the car's tinted glass and the torrential rain: a wall separating him from any unlikely pedestrians.

It won't be easy to arrange so many banknotes in a single suitcase, however large it may be. He will procrastinate as he divides and joins the bundles of notes, but eventually the job of decanting them will be complete. Anyone walking past the entrance to Palacio Salvo half an hour later will see a man approach in a hurry, dragging a suitcase across the wet paving stones. His clothes are soaked with sweat and rain; his eyes sunken, he has the slightly lost look of one on the edge of exhaustion. Even observing him from afar we would recognize a man who is over the hill without ever having been at his peak. However, if we look at him more closely, we can see that there is, on his face, a satisfied smirk. His mind seems to be elsewhere, he does not appear bothered by his wet clothes, perhaps he is mentally reviewing his plans.

At this time of day, the lobby is full of people hurrying to and fro. Diego looks at the guy on duty, someone he has never seen before, although there is nothing unusual about that, given the high turnover at companies that provide cleaners and security staff.

He doesn't greet anybody and nobody greets him, nobody looks at him or recognizes him, nobody notices his luggage. Lots of people are coming and going to the apartments, offices and stores. He crosses the space, heads for one of the elevators and gets in with two teenage girls, who laugh, chat and check their phones while fluttering their eyelashes.

Diego gets out first, and the sound of the metal grille closing behind him brings to an end the adventure of transporting the money from the heist to his new apartment. He walks down a long corridor and opens the door of the rented place; he lets go of the suitcase, carefully locks the door behind him and bolts it for extra reassurance; he leans against the timber and rests for a second. And he closes his eyes.

The apartment is smaller and darker than his own, the windows of its gloomy living room open onto an air shaft that never sees the sun. He doesn't mind it being dark in the middle of the day, as if the belly of the building protects him from the threats of the outside world.

Diego takes off his coat, hangs it over the back of a chair and looks for the bathroom; he discovers it behind the second door, opens the tap and lets the water run until it is warm. When it is tepid, he splashes it on his face and neck, allows it to run over his wrists, then dries himself with a clean towel. He leans on the edge of the basin and sees his face in the mirror, a face that speaks of a difficult day. He recalls the heist, the explosions, the death and destruction unleashed by the Hobo, his eyes bloodshot with cocaine and violence, the shouts, the bullets fired at innocent people.

He remembers when Ursula appeared, just when the Hobo was about to kill him, remembers as if in a dream how she shot the Hobo, how they fled together before the police arrived: Ursula, him and the money.

Now he is holed up here, a place nobody else knows about, somewhere he has rented under another name. He begins to feel safe, he begins to feel at peace. He hears a dog barking in the distance, the desperate howl of a caged animal, the sound so distant it is as if it is coming from another world.

He opens the tap again, rolls up his sleeves, allows the water to run, splashes more on his cheeks. Gradually, his tired face dissolves into a satisfied expression. She arrived when she needed to, did what she needed to, shot the person she needed to. She told him the Hobo was a bad person. Or something like that, he doesn't quite remember.

The barking grows louder, more desperate. Poor beast, perhaps it's locked into a small apartment like this one, or even in the kitchen or the bathroom, somewhere that would be a prison for the animal.

Diego feels an enormous sense of gratitude towards the woman. So why did he leave her alone, just a few hours after the heist? Why did he flee with all the money? He tries to justify himself: he was paralysed by the fear that the police were combing the city. He was terrified of returning to prison, the panic attacks left him with no option but to escape and take refuge at home. He didn't intend to make off with the money, he simply wanted to get away and the money was incidental: it sat in the back of the car until the next day.

He was lucky to recover it.

His body is still tense, as if he has narrowly escaped an accident. He still looks gaunt and pale, but the colour is starting to come back to his cheeks. He no longer feels as if he is about to faint, his teeth are no longer chattering. He looks at the suitcase, thinks about the money inside. For the first time in a long time, and for various reasons which we have neither the capacity nor the wish to analyse, Diego is beginning to feel okay.

He comes out of the bathroom and looks for the bedroom that contains the closet he saw on the website: fortunately, it is as large as it looked in the photos, wide enough to accommodate a huge suitcase, and with a proper lock.

Diego opens the case, takes out a bundle of notes wrapped in thermo-sealed plastic, and places it in the drawer of the nightstand. Then he puts the suitcase in the closet.

He stands back, observes his work. He moves it half an inch, turns the key, then attaches the key to a fob, which he puts in his trouser pocket. For now, this is all he can do: hide himself, hide the money. Later on, he will see. Right now, he's going to rest, keep a watch on his apartment – which is two floors higher up – and wait. He won't leave the building again any time soon. He'll order in from a bar: a breaded cutlet, some fries, a Coca-Cola. Perhaps some crème caramel.

And tomorrow will be another day.

X

Antinucci is standing in the middle of Plaza Matriz. The final note of a piece by Mozart, played by a street violinist, leaves him silent and blinking with emotion.

Such is the delicious power of music. Around him, the audience disperses, their words and cries sullying a perfect moment. He could barely breathe as he listened to the end of the requiem. Standing there, he realized that a day that began with that piece could only be an auspicious one, and now we see him take out a banknote, which he will drop into the musician's hat before continuing on his way.

He is briefly overcome with a sense of well-being, almost of happiness, a sense that begins to dissipate with the frantic noise of the city. He will focus again on the tasks on his list.

Antinucci crosses the intricate maze of the Old Town, lost in thought, in a single all-encompassing thought. He is formally dressed, his shoes look Italian, he wears an elegantly tailored blue suit, the kind of clothes that immediately call to mind words such as *executive* or *lawyer*. However, when he enters a space, the word we think of is *sinister*.

He can't stop thinking about the woman who appeared at the hold-up, who shot the Hobo, who ran off with Diego and the money.

Who she is, where she came from and, above all, where the devil she is now. From morning to night her face has become an obsession, occupying almost all his thoughts, like a girlfriend, like a lover, like his mother. But she is a thief who made off with the money, all the money from the robbery he had planned, he had organized, he had supervised. How did she get away? How did she manage it?

He knows that if he wants to put his ideas in order, he has to start at the beginning.

Everything got off on the wrong foot: he didn't have the right people, ones up to the job of robbing a cash truck, and the crew he had recruited had no experience: not Skinflint, not Diego, a couple of two-bit crooks, a pickpocket and a wannabe kidnapper he had sprung from prison on the condition that he take part in this heist. And the Hobo... but better not to think about that psychotic murderer or the trail of corpses he left at the scene of what was meant to be a simple robbery.

Antinucci remembers, and he starts to sweat; despite the cold, despite the freezing wind, the drops of perspiration run down his neck. He starts to feel dirty, and he hates feeling dirty. His moist lower lip contracts into a grimace that, even from a distance, is disturbing. He also hates the winter, the nights when the sky is white with cold, the trees black and bare, the streets wet even when it hasn't rained. He hates this climate that makes the buildings of this part of the Old Town look a little more run down in the misty light, a little older and shabbier, like a piece of furniture left out on the street since last summer.

As he walks, he avoids the puddles of dirty water at the corners, the broken paving stones, the plastic bags flapping in the wind.

He arrives at a door in Calle Treinta y Tres, number 333, a building that looks like so many others, neglected, on the verge of being abandoned. He rings the bell. He allows thirty seconds to pass, a minute, then rings again. Footsteps approach, a lad opens the door, looks at him, says nothing.

"Good afternoon, young man. I was looking for the master – or the mistress – of this house."

"What do you want?"

"I'm looking for a lady, a woman I saw a couple of days ago entering the door on the right, which I think leads to your garage."

The lad gives no sign of understanding; he gives no sign of anything at all, and Antinucci thinks how little he knows about the woman he is looking for, just that she had the key to the garage of this house. Is she the owner, a friend, maybe someone who rents some space?

"Maybe I should explain. I saw a woman go through that door. She was in her forties, plump, with light brown hair. Do you know who I'm talking about? I need to find her."

He looks up, trying to see inside the house. A corridor with chequerboard tiles, a glazed door, an armchair covered with clothes, signs of the disorder and untidiness to be found in the homes of the younger generations, God have mercy on us. Nothing that could be linked to the woman.

The lad makes no gesture, doesn't say a word, simply looks back in silence, his expression vacuous or vaguely bad-tempered.

"I don't know if the woman I'm talking about is the owner or…" Antinucci leaves the conjunction floating in the air, hoping to elicit something. So far, the lad hasn't said a word.

"No, the owner is a friend."

"So you don't know a woman who has the key to the garage? Perhaps he lets her use it."

"Haven't a clue. I only arrived this morning."

"Could I talk to the owner then?"

"No. He left a couple of hours ago, and he's going to be away all month."

Antinucci feels that the virus of catastrophe, until now a latent threat, has burst onto the scene. "Is there any way to get in touch with him? Phone? Email?"

"No."

"It's important."

"If it's so important, tell me what it's about."

The words sound aggressive. Now the lad looks him up and down, assessing him with a mixture of curiosity and mistrust. The conversation is a static, shapeless thing, one in which Antinucci bears all the weight, and the signs of failure are clear in each of his questions. The lawyer has to make an effort to contain the spasmodic desire to strike the lad right between the eyes or to split his lip; and he also feels an almost physical need to get away, to run to his car and return home. He swallows his pride and plays his last card.

"I assure you that it is very important I locate that woman or talk to the owner because —"

The young man raises his hand in a gesture that has the symbolic power to interrupt the lawyer's sentence. "I already told you the owner left. Who are you, anyway?"

"An acquaintance of the woman I was telling you about."

"So why are you looking for the owner?"

"To ask him how to find her. When did he leave?"

"I already told you he left a couple of hours ago. To a spiritual retreat in Brazil, no phone, no computer. You understand, amigo?"

Antinucci doesn't know what to do now, he hadn't foreseen this possibility. He feels like grabbing the little bastard by his hair and slamming his face into the wall. Cracking every single one of his goddamn teeth on the door frame. Sinking a knee into his fucking balls. Instead, he gives an almost obsequious smile.

"Okay. I'll be back in a month. Thanks for your help, young man."

The lad shuts the door without a word, and the lawyer stands looking at the worm-eaten wood as he swallows his anger. He takes out a cigarette, places it between his lips, looks for the gold cigarette lighter, puts away the cigarette again, curses, restrains himself.

He takes the same route towards the square, where he left his car. Just then it starts to rain, and the umbrellas of the passers-by begin to open.

How he loathes the arrogance of youth. When he was young, people had values, respect. He curses, this time without remorse.

XI

I don't know how Luz got my details. An acquaintance had supposedly given her my name and address but she didn't remember who it was, and that struck me as strange, yet not so strange as to make me refuse to accept the case. When she turned up here, she was expecting a man…

I'd just spent a month on the trail of an unfaithful husband, an older man, financially comfortable, who had disappeared three weeks earlier, his wife informed me. The police search had produced no results, time was passing, and there were no signs of his whereabouts. The man had vanished into thin air, something one might have thought impossible in the era of social media and smartphones. But he had disappeared, his track going cold at the border crossing with Brazil, and at first it had been impossible to find so much as a single clue. However, after four weeks of bribing police officers, offering rewards and receiving false information, I tracked him down to a luxury hotel by a beach paradise, in the predictable company of a young woman and, equally predictably, with enough money in his bank account to pay for those hotels and those women for the rest of his existence.

His wife seemed relieved when she heard my report (I think it meant she became chair of her husband's companies); she paid my fees and added a generous and above all unexpected bonus for my work. At the precise moment Luz knocked on my door, I had been about to leave and take a vacation with my unforeseen income.

As soon as she entered my office, I registered the concern on the face of this woman in her early forties, with her beautiful features and her expensive clothes; I heard the anxiety of unvoiced suspicions, her reluctance to speak clearly. Perhaps I intuited the existence of a family drama deeper and more terrible than the mere disappearance of a ring or the woman's mysterious encounter with Ursula on a rainy night. Whatever the reason – maybe I was seduced by the doubt and hesitation, by this tale of sisters with a crime (or two) in the mix – I decided to postpone my trip and I accepted the case.

Moreover, the job would help me to push aside the confusion I had been struggling with, ever since the end of my relationship with another woman. Although it had been a brief relationship and was already over, it had shaken my foundations.

I didn't know any more about Luz López other than the obvious: she was rich, she spent more on sunglasses than I spent on my entire wardrobe, she ate frugally, she put in a lot of hours at the gym, and she had the most beautiful eyes I had ever seen. Despite this, she did not seem to fit entirely into the stereotype of the beautiful wife; there was something more, a certain intelligence, an instinctive brilliance perhaps.

When I saw her enter, I thought to myself that beauty was not the only attribute of this woman who had come to my office, full of doubt and suspicion, to ask me to investigate her sister, her beloved sister. She didn't seem at ease, sitting in front of me, on the other side of my desk. She seemed tense, her guard was up, but nobody is comfortable when they come to see me for the first time and they have to discuss problems that are awkward or difficult to explain to a stranger.

It was easy to find out all about Luz, the person I was working for: she had been the rich wife of the man she was divorcing in order to marry someone else, an even richer man.

Some of them are like that, beautiful women who go from one level of wealth to the next, almost as if it were a well-paid job in which they are regularly promoted. However, I couldn't help thinking Luz didn't fit into that category, or at least that it wasn't all there was to her.

I was unsure whether to accept the case.

In the end – why deny it? – I was swayed by the aura of attraction that surrounds rich, beautiful women. And I accepted the investigation. But I still don't know much about the enigma called Ursula. The public information about her gets mixed up with information about another woman who has the same name. Actually, I should say who *had* the same name, because the other Ursula died; she was murdered a little over a month ago, in circumstances that are unclear.

And as far as Ursula López goes – the one who's alive, the one I'm investigating – there is hardly any information. And this lack of information can only be due to two reasons: either her life is unremarkable, or someone has deliberately erased the information. So far, I'm inclined to go with the former of the two possibilities.

All I've managed to discover after personally putting her under surveillance is that just about the only time she leaves home is to attend a therapy meeting, like Alcoholics Anonymous but for fat people: every Wednesday she takes the bus to a church in Punta Carretas, where a dozen overweight people get together and talk about how overweight they are.

The sister mentioned that she's a translator, she works from home and leads a quiet life, a boring one even. Maybe that explains everything.

Or almost everything. Because yesterday I discovered something unusual about her: she's being tailed by a policewoman. I know the spy is a policewoman because I followed her. I know she works at police headquarters, in Calle San José. I've tried all my contacts in the force, but I haven't managed to find out what Captain Leonilda Lima is investigating or why she's following Ursula López, whose name doesn't figure in any of the cases assigned to Lima. I'm starting to wonder whether Captain Leonilda Lima is following Ursula for personal reasons. Yes. Any investigation can bring dirt to the surface, reveal monsters hiding inside insignificant people, throw up brutal surprises, and I'm starting to suspect this will be no exception.

XII

Ursula swore on her life that she knew nothing about the murder of Auntie Irene; that, when she arrived that afternoon, Irene was already dead. She told me the ring had turned up one day when she was cleaning the house, which has been locked up ever since the day of the crime.

For some reason I didn't believe her. I'm not sure how I'd answer if anyone asked me whether I thought she was capable of something evil, of something sordid.

I know my sister sometimes loses control and unleashes earthquakes. And there's more. Auntie Irene was always tyrannical, vindictive, even malevolent towards her; and, looking back, I think she hated her niece. And I suspect that, later on, when Ursula was older, my aunt began to fear her.

I wonder what really went on between them. But whether she was innocent or guilty of whatever happened, something changed after Irene's murder, after that terrible afternoon when the maid's boyfriend shot her in her sleep. My sister became more distant, more closed in on herself, she seemed dissatisfied, her personality became darker: a metal curtain came down, and she became distant, inaccessible, opaque.

———

I remember our childhood, when we were a normal family, happy. Were we ever a happy family? Were we at least normal? Now I suspect we were neither. I remember – and above all, Ursula remembers – Daddy's punishments, the penances he imposed on her for stealing food from the fridge:

"One day of punishment, Ursula. No light and no food. The darkness will make you strong, fasting will cleanse your body."

When morning came and Daddy released her, Ursula was transformed, her eyes looked different when she came out of her bedroom, there was a glint of madness, something that would grow and become more visible with time.

I particularly remember one morning when Daddy had opened my sister's bedroom door, released her from captivity and then left for work. Ursula and I were doing our homework at the kitchen table, on the check tablecloth. Our jotters, books and pencils covered most of the surface. Her face was an enigma, a mask of tranquillity: her lips were straight, like a line cutting her face in two.

We had a cook at home, and we called her the watchwoman because we knew she spied on us, reporting Ursula's raids on the fridge. My sister, always so hungry, always in search of something more to swallow; and the watchwoman, a hateful person who more than once had told tales to Daddy.

Although I never saw the cook again after that day, I still remember her well: dumpy, wheezing, with a sarcastic smile.

She said something to Ursula, I don't remember what, something about the punishment from which Daddy had just released her, in a mocking tone. My sister grunted, a sound I had never heard her make, a low noise as if coming from a deep well, and her mask cracked. It was replaced by a look of rage, like a wounded animal.

I didn't notice she had grabbed the metal compasses she had been using for her geometry homework; she jumped to her feet and stabbed them into the watchwoman's arm not once but three times, in quick succession. I jumped up too, grabbed my sister's sleeve to stop her hand, to stop her.

Ursula's grunt was followed immediately by a series of disconnected sounds: the woman's screams of pain, the chair clattering over, a body sliding to the floor. I tried to shout, but all I could produce was a strangled croak. The red stain began to slide down the cook's arm, to drip onto the linoleum, forming a puddle.

My sister threw away the compasses, returned to her chair, restored her mask of tranquillity. A strange expression slid over her face, like a hand in a stolen glove. She shook her head slowly, with that calm, expressionless face, betrayed only by the sweat on her brow and the tendons of her neck. Her movements reflected not rage but rather disgust or aversion, and of the three of us she was the only one who didn't lose her calm.

The scene is frozen in my memory: the watchwoman on the floor, the red stain on the linoleum, the sharp cries, Ursula's tranquillity, time transformed into a solid entity.

I don't remember what happened next; I've forgotten or I got my timeline mixed up. I know that at some point Daddy arrived with a doctor and that the watchwoman disappeared from our house for good. And I remember something else, although I might have dreamed it or made it up. One day, shortly after, Daddy put his hand on my shoulder and spoke to me in a low voice, so she couldn't hear.

"Your sister is a black hole, Luz. You're going to have to look after her."

"And if that isn't enough?"

He glanced nervously towards Ursula's room. "I don't know, Luz, I don't know."

The past slots each memory into its place and there it remains, growing and shrinking, waxing and waning, but never disappearing completely. Thinking about that moment with Daddy makes me question whether the dialogue ever took place, and the unease sends me in search of other clues about Ursula.

I stop somewhere between that yesterday and now, I search for information, I investigate. Because who can doubt that an invisible thread links the past to the present? Some questions are like holes, like wells that can never be filled.

That's why I went to see the detective, that's why I asked her to investigate what my sister does, apart from translating poetry and going to self-help meetings for the obese. If I already suspected she needed my help, now I'm sure. And how can I help you, Ursula, sister darling, if I sometimes feel as if I hardly recognize you? Dear God, I think, how can I help her?

God, as usual, does not answer.

I'm going to see her at lunchtime, and I'll try to speak to her. To get inside her, to access her dark side. Because it's like Daddy said: my sister is a black hole.

XIII

It's a beautiful winter afternoon in Montevideo and, at least for now, the clear sky recalls a perfectly ironed light blue sheet.

The two pairs of feet walk or slide across the parquet floor and stop at the entrance to the dining room; the feet on the right are sheathed in something low and comfortable, what we might define as dressy sneakers or posh sports shoes, while the feet on the left are in a pair of black patent leather stilettos, a very popular model this winter for those with calves of steel and who are foolhardy enough to brave four-inch heels.

Both pairs of feet – the ones on the left and those on the right – are led inside by a third pair, which we do not need to describe. They reach the table at the window, the best in the place.

Luz and Ursula regularly meet up at this restaurant, a place neither so vulgar as to make Luz feel uncomfortable nor so posh that Ursula cannot pay her way, something she insists on doing despite the fact that her sister is both rich and generous.

They glance at the menu, call the waitress and order their food: the girl leaves, and the women's eyes meet for an instant then go their separate ways and survey the other tables.

A John Lennon song is playing, one of those catchy tunes from the period when he was a pacifist and they took photos of him in bed with Yoko Ono. Luz hums along.

Through the window, Ursula watches the sky floating by, a sky that five minutes ago was light blue but is now flecked with long cotton clouds through which shine rays of sunlight, the sort of vision that must have inspired Joaquín Suárez, the governor who created the Uruguayan flag. She listens to her sister humming, and she smiles at her patiently, lovingly. Luz returns the smile, though she seems to think twice before she speaks.

"Are you going to the cemetery one of these days, Ursula?"

"What a coincidence. I was just thinking about going either this week or next."

"It's about time you took flowers to Mummy, Daddy and Auntie Irene. I know it sounds odd, but it's very peaceful there."

"There's no need to go on about it: I don't believe in all these rituals around death. But you're right, this time I'm going to go, I've got to go. Even if it's only the once."

"Well, whatever you think, a visit on a beautiful sunny day can't do you any harm. Do you have the keys to the mausoleum? I mean, if you're going you can check everything's okay."

"Yes. You've got one and I've got the other. Daddy made sure we had one each. Because Daddy thought of everything, didn't he?"

Luz half closes her eyes, inspects the back of her hands. She doesn't answer.

"This morning I was thinking about old family stories, Luz, the way relationships can be so crazy and twisted, especially between sisters."

"I think about that all the time. A love–hate relationship?"

Ursula considers the idea while she dips a piece of bread in some salsa. "Is that how you see it? I don't agree. I think there's a connection between us. Sometimes it's stronger and sometimes it's weaker, but it's always there, indestructible."

"I've never hated you, Ursula, even if sometimes I don't understand you."

"You can always ask, and I can always decide how to answer."

Luz seems to consider the suggestion, her right hand toying with the paper napkin and the fork. "I'm going to take you at your word and start right now. Is that okay?"

"I guess I don't have any choice."

"What happened to Auntie Irene? Is there something you haven't told me?"

This question, posed in a non-committal, almost casual tone, shakes Ursula from her complacency. She looks at Luz with the distant concentration she sometimes dedicates to food she is about to swallow.

The waitress's feet approach across the parquet floor, stand still for a second in front of the table, move around it from one side to the other. Time is suspended, petrified, impassive, and Ursula's response only comes when the feet have begun their return journey, away from the table.

"I don't know exactly what your suspicions are, Luz. Why do you think I know a different version to the official one?"

"I never believed what you told me about how the ring turned up by chance."

There is a moment of silence.

"Do you think I killed Auntie Irene and stole the ring?"

"No. That's not it. But I know you didn't like her, and I know sometimes your dislikes take a violent turn."

"That's a hard thing to hear from my own sister."

"And it's hard to say, I can assure you."

Ursula attacks her sirloin steak with fries, adds mustard, corrects the seasoning, tastes it, and seems satisfied. She cuts another piece, and another, raises the fork to her mouth, chews. The plate is not very large, these set lunches with their portion control; she finishes after little more than five minutes of methodical, conscientious chewing. She swallows the last chunk of meat with mustard and two French fries, mops the plate with a piece of bread, cleans her mouth with the napkin. Luz hasn't touched her grilled cod, hasn't taken her eyes off her sister.

Ursula raises her wine glass. "A toast, Luz. Leaving aside all your suspicions, leaving aside my supposed violence, you are the person I love most in the world."

Her sister hesitates, looks away, and just then the angle at which the light hits the window changes, transforming it into a mirror: she sees herself, sees Ursula turn her head, and their eyes meet in the glass.

Luz raises her glass to the reflected image. "Here's to our eyes meeting outside of the world of mirrors."

Ursula drinks. She knows time is running out, that the truth will carve a path between them sooner or later. She wonders if she should tell her everything now or wait, perhaps order something more to eat.

"I could dodge your questions, Luz, but I'm tired."

In silence and to herself, she promises Luz she will be totally honest, that she won't put it off any longer. But she can't do it today, or at least she can't tell her the whole truth today. She places the glass on the tablecloth, leaving her hands free, her fingers interlaced as they rest on the table.

"Where did it all start? It's hard to define a beginning, the moment the seeds were planted. Was it now, two months ago, forty years ago?"

"I'm getting scared now. This sounds serious."

"It is. One night, a couple of months ago, I received a phone call meant for somebody else, and it changed my life."

"That's a good start to a story. I think I've read it somewhere before. *City of Glass*, by Paul Auster? Sorry, I didn't mean to interrupt."

"As a result of the call I met a man, and the man led me into situations I'd never been in before."

"I don't know what you're talking about. What kind of situations do you mean?"

Ursula's fingers separate, extend, her hands look rigid, the palms resting on the surface of the table. "Holding up an armoured truck."

Caught up as they are in their own concerns, they both have the intuition that something momentous is about to happen, and the silence that follows takes a different form in each of them. A sigh, a cold breath, creeps up Luz's spine; a heaviness settles on Ursula's eyelids.

"You took part in the heist that was in the news?"

"Not exactly. I wasn't there during the hold-up. I arrived on the scene at the end, when almost everything had already happened and… It's impossible to explain what it was like, it was a battlefield, a massacre."

———

Let us focus on Luz's face. We are in no condition to say whether her astonishment is born of horror or incredulity, but as she listens to her sister the expression on her face changes by the second. Her voice is barely audible.

"And…?"

"The man I told you about, the one I met by mistake, the one who'd called me, I got him into a van and I fled with him and the cash from the heist."

"You took the money from a robbery?"

"Yes. I ran off with the loot."

There is another long, heavy silence, one of those pauses that arise in the midst of a confession when the revelation is serious and unexpected: decades of infidelity, a mis-attributed paternity, or that one's sister, a translator by profession, has fled with the money from a heist.

"I can't believe it, Ursula. I can't believe it."

"You suspected something was up, and you weren't wrong."

"And now you have all that money?"

Ursula thinks about how to explain the thorny issue of the money to her sister. As she thinks, she looks for the waitress, signals to her, orders another portion of what she has just had, but with roast potatoes and salad. And a cheese souf-flé. With plenty of pepper. When she turns her head, Luz is still looking at her.

"Not right now. I'll have it in a few days. My partner and I have hidden the money."

"Where?"

"I can't tell you, Luz. It's for your own safety. Excuse me, could you bring me a slice of quiche? And a portion of the mushrooms in cream sauce. I don't care if it's not part of the set lunch."

The waitress leaves.

"Holding up an armoured truck. I can't believe it, Ursula. You took part in a heist on an armoured truck."

To Luz, it is all as strange as if a polar bear had walked into the restaurant and sat down at their table.

XIV

Antinucci wears his Ray-Bans when driving, even on cloudy days. A large part of his life takes part behind dark glass, and although he says it's due to his sensitivity to light, we suspect that his real intention is to hide his eyes, which are large, bulging, with fleshy lids. Eyes that, if not exactly ugly, have something unpleasant about them, something he tries to conceal behind the wall of his tinted lenses.

Strangely, he is not listening to music, and an unusual silence reigns inside the car, an Audi A6 that still smells like new, a vehicle only a couple of months old. The Bullet, as he calls it, must have cost a fortune, although nobody can imagine how much he paid to have it brought direct from Germany, equipped with all the latest high-tech accessories and upholstered in real leather.

On the dashboard he has erected a small altar, very discreet: a couple of images of the Virgin Mary, a medallion of St Christopher bearing the Infant on his shoulder (a gift from his beloved mother). And a rosary of mother-of-pearl beads blessed by the Pope – the previous incumbent, not the current one, obviously – hangs from the rear-view mirror. Our lawyer, who, in addition to being crazy about top-of-the-range automobiles, is also a music lover with exquisite taste and a fine ear, commissioned the best audio system for his vehicle. However, as we were saying, today he is not listening to his customary baroque music, and the car progresses in silence.

He is headed for the church of Las Esclavas del Sagrado Corazón, and thinks that it is two days since he last smoked, that he has several small acupuncture needles embedded behind his ear, and that his cravings have been receding for some time, perhaps two or three hours. The method, they told him before charging him fifteen hundred dollars, is based on the belief that the body depends on flows of energy along the meridians on which the acupuncture points are located. The needles, they explained after putting away the money and without the slightest suggestion they would give him a receipt, far less an invoice, would divert this flow towards a specific part of the body, re-establishing equilibrium, eliminating anxiety and deactivating nervous states. Or something like that.

Antinucci turns onto Calle Ellauri, knowing that at this time of day finding a parking place is going to be hell.

He furrows his brow; he is unsure whether these oriental beliefs are a form of superstition, whether they represent a vision that contradicts the revelation of Jesus Christ Our Saviour. He should not forget or underestimate the constant action of the father of lies (John 8:44), of the Devil who, as the Scriptures tell us, seeks to divert man from truth and lead him into evil (1 Peter 5:8), despite the defeat inflicted on him when the Son of God came into the world (Philippians 2:9–11).

The lawyer sighs. For now he decides not to consult Father Ismael because he fears his remonstrances; he will decide whether to tell him about it later, at confession, once the needles have had a chance to do their work. But

99

for the moment he can't even contemplate weighing up the guilt of believing in the magical effect of the pinpricks; he has more than enough with the matter that has brought him to church on a day when he doesn't normally visit the confessional.

Antinucci is not at peace. As he drives, the word *sin* bounces around inside his head. The idea that he might be offending God makes him feel dirty, blemished, but does not diminish his hatred towards that woman, his wish to see her suffer, his desire to hurt her.

He needs to confess, urgently. Afterwards, God willing, he will perform whatever penitence Father Ismael imposes, he will say his Our Father, his Hail Mary, his Glory Be, and everything will return to its former tranquillity.

When he finds a space he thinks it's a good omen, a sign that Divine Providence is ready to forgive him. He parks, taking the utmost care not to scratch the paintwork of his beloved car. He steps out and feels a sense of mild optimism, despite the sin that refuses to relent, the wrath that stubbornly remains.

Father Ismael will know what to advise; and, despite the weight of his offence, Antinucci feels a certain joy that prefigures his future sanctification. He examines his conscience and is annoyed, time and time again, to be brought up short by his rage, by his desire to punch that face until it is a mass of bloody flesh.

As Antinucci makes his way towards the church, a distance of some two hundred yards, which he covers with a springy stride, we may say that this man received the sacrament of baptism at the age of three months, to judge by a photo (black and white, on thick grainy paper) that hangs on the wall above his desk at home, the date handwritten in blue ink. In the photo is a baby in a long lacy gown, trimmed with tucks and ruffles; and although the infant is bald, without the slightest trace of the hair that today is combed and gelled, the eyes already betray a certain peculiarity; they are large, bulging, the lids too fleshy, and leave not the slightest margin of doubt as to his identity.

Antinucci was christened, we were saying; and ever since he became a child of God by grace, and a member of the Holy Catholic Church, our lawyer has been a faithful adherent of his religion, one might even say a fanatical one. He knows that contrition is essential to penance, that there must be a clear and decisive rejection of sin, born of one's love of God. However, he also knows that, to confess, it is sufficient to show attrition, an imperfect repentance owing more to the fear of God than to the love one professes for Him. And this time, as so many times before, he will have to rely on attrition.

He reaches the church, lowers his head, crosses himself in an expansive movement that goes from the crown of his head to somewhere down near his navel, and from the outside of his left shoulder to his right; then he heads for the confessional.

Nobody is waiting. He kneels, speaks to a face that is veiled behind the latticed panel. "In the name of the Father, the Son and the Holy Ghost."

The priest clears his throat. "May the Lord be in your heart so that you may repent and humbly confess your sins."

"It has been five days since my last confession."

"How have you sinned?"

"I want to hurt a woman, Father. I want to cause her pain."

"Perhaps you're angry. That often happens."

"I dream that I'm hurting her, that I'm torturing her with terrible implements."

There is a hesitation, a second in which Father Ismael seems to lose his aura of sanctity, seems to forget the script, is disoriented; but he's a professional, he's seen it all or, rather, he's heard it all, sitting in this seat of his.

"And you have repented of these feelings but they return?"

"No, Father Ismael, I have not repented. I can't stop thinking about making her suffer."

"You don't feel the pain of contrition."

"No, and I can't make it stop."

"However, there is attrition, an imperfect contrition, and that too is a gift from God. If there were no attrition you would not be here."

"Yes, Father Ismael."

"You must strive to achieve contrition, and in the meantime you will pray your penitence."

"Yes, Father Ismael."

Antinucci listens to the priest, hears his advice and his recommendations. He listens to the voice that will soothe him, if only for a few days, the voice that elevates him to a state of sanctity, even though he knows he is not confessing everything.

"God, merciful Father who reconciled himself with the world through the death and resurrection of his Son and poured out the Holy Spirit for the remission of sin, grants you, through the ministry of the Church, forgiveness and peace. And I absolve you of your sins, in the name of the Father, the Son and the Holy Ghost."

Antinucci says "amen" and stands up.

But today, grace is not working as it did on other occasions. He leaves the church; inside his pockets he tenses his fingers, opening and closing them, squeezing them tight, as if he was breaking something, throttling it. He gets into the car, swipes the rosary from the rear-view mirror; says a short prayer, "Blessed be the Holy and Immaculate Conception of the Virgin Mary, Mother of God"; brings the beads to his mouth and presses his lips against them and then against the St Christopher. "Blessed be the Holy and Immaculate Conception of the Virgin Mary, Mother of God," he murmurs, again and again, closing his eyes and kissing the pearly beads, wetting them one by one with his saliva. He looks at the image of Mary, kisses it with unction. "Blessed be the Holy and Immaculate Conception of the Virgin Mary, Mother of God." He licks it, puts it in his mouth and sucks it, sucks the image of the Virgin and his voice becomes louder, he is shouting, the tears falling onto his lapels.

XV

Are you in a bad mood, Ursula? Were you disturbed by the voices of the dead? Did you wake up with grey bags under your eyes? Were you bitten by mosquitoes, tarantulas, vipers? Did you sleep badly and have nightmares? Was your neighbour walking back and forth, her heels hammering into your skull?

Does the noise of the world refuse to leave you in peace? How long have you been having these nightmares? Are you hungry? Did you wake up and go to the fridge? Were you thinking about the money you stole and still haven't recovered? Are they stopping you from sleeping in the house in Carrasco, stopping you from getting that car? Do you think about Luz's house, her car? About your undying love for your sister? About your weight? Are you in a bad mood, Ursula?

Did the dead speak to you all night long? Did you think about all your abandoned translations? About the laundry basket now full to overflowing? About Diego?

Or about the money? Perhaps you're trying to come up with another lie to tell in your therapy group? Do you tell lies all mixed up with reality? Do you ask yourself why you chose this life?

Do you ask yourself if this is all you deserve? Do you deserve this house you've inherited, the rugs you didn't choose, the Japanese figurines you didn't clean this Sunday or the one before? Do you remember the last time you cleaned them?

Why do you live in this apartment? Why don't you go somewhere else, somewhere without memories? Why didn't you leave long ago? Are you thinking about Diego? What are you going to do with the money from the robbery? Are you going to lose weight, become somebody different? Another house and another life?

Do you recall the dead or do you let them invade you?

Are you going to continue to allow them to live for you? Are you in a bad mood, Ursula? What shape does your life have? Does your life have a shape?

Do you add up all the time you wasted cleaning Daddy's Japanese figurines? And dieting? Why do you keep that old furniture? The worn curtains, the shabby armchairs? Why are you so angry?

Are you hungry? Hungry enough to eat a whole leg of ham, to wolf down a jar of jam and a gallon of ice cream?

Do you walk and try not to tread on the cracks between the paving stones? Why don't things work out the way they should? How should things work out, Ursula? Do you think about Diego? Or about the money? About being fat? About getting rid of that layer of adipose tissue covering your body? Or about eating?

Do you see ghosts? Do you know how to forgive?

When you remember the past, does it make you angry? Do you remember the girl you used to be? Do you want to forget her? Have you already thrown up your breakfast? Are you hungry again? Do you think about the obligation to be thin and rich and elegant, and all the damn restrictions in your life? Are you a pervert who spies on people?

A fantasist? A compulsive eater? A thief? Are they going to throw you to the lions when they find you out? Are they going to burn you at the stake? Do you ever really repent? Do you keep going, despite everything? How does it feel when you kill? Does the blood of your rage heal you? Are you hungry? Do you hear voices that never stop talking? Are you in a bad mood, darling Ursula?

THE ESCAPE

Ursula resists the temptation to look back; she pushes Luz through the jaws of the tunnel, which close behind them. They crawl forward, knees and palms on the floor. Luz goes ahead, her way lit by Ursula's flashlight. And, now we think about it, why does Ursula have such a powerful flashlight in her bag?

The space is narrow, a passageway dug into the earth. The roof is too low for them to stand, too low even to crouch; the gallery is only slightly wider than their bodies.

Ursula feels the fear clinging to her clothes, in her sweat, in her throat; the fear is mingled with anxiety and also with excitement. Perhaps she should not have chosen this means of escape, but she did and there's no turning back now.

Luz was crying at the start, but no longer. Ursula has a revolver in the pink bag squeezed beneath her arm.

For the first few yards they feel as if they are suffocating, more due to the psychological effect of confinement than from a shortage of oxygen because the tunnel, we know, has a ventilation pipe.

They feel their way along the walls; the floor and ceiling are uneven and stony, damp as if water was leaking in. Above is Montevideo, a sad, melancholic city with beautiful beaches and the narrow-minded customs of a small town.

Above is Montevideo, a gentle, friendly city, green and hospitable, a city that, when it reveals its underbelly and its sewers, can be a very frightening place.

Above, unheard by them, the city's incessant noise and its incessant cruelty rumble on.

They crawl in silence, advancing with difficulty. Their senses gradually adapt to the confinement, the suffocating sensation begins to fade. They don't talk, each is locked in her thoughts.

As the euphoria of the events they have been through up there dissipates, Ursula thinks about the money from the hold-up, she thinks about all that money. *It's my money, Daddy, be quiet.*

Imagine a gallery scarcely higher than your body, a narrow tunnel with no end in sight. Think about the sense of suffocation that comes from being buried alive deep in the belly of the earth, entombed in a long black hole, with the sensation that there are several yards of earth and asphalt and buildings above your head.

They aren't cowards, they don't easily fall victim to fear, but how can they stop themselves thinking about the fact that the slightest slip, the merest movement could make this place into a tomb, their tomb? A fatal movement that they themselves could set off.

A WEEK
BEFORE THE ESCAPE

I

I've asked myself a thousand times why I don't call Diego and put an end to this anxious waiting that's been going on for almost a month. But no, I wait and I wait, even though I'm not sure what I'm waiting for or why. The phone is like a dead mouse, abandoned on the pillow, here at my side.

I spend too much time in bed, waiting for something to happen even though it never does, and my patience is in shreds, moth-eaten, riddled with holes. I still don't want to think about it, even though I know it's possible Diego will never call, that I'll lose my share of the money, that I'll have to report the theft of my VW Golf: the threat hangs over my head.

I could turn on the television and lose myself in one of those programmes on which people compete to see who the best cook is, who the best dancer is, who can come up with the most scandalous piece of gossip, I could watch one of those programmes people never own up to watching while, behind closed doors, they lap up every last titillating drop. But no, I prefer to wallow in this sense of abandonment, to feel wretched, to wait and hope, to suffer as a result of the disappearance of Diego, of my money, of my car. And sometimes I decide to be trusting and optimistic, to dream about the new life awaiting me, to lose myself in the hope of change.

That's what I'm doing, trying to decide on my state of mind, and the ringtone is mixed up with my fantasies, with one of my thousand wishes, with one of my self-fulfilling prophecies. However, it turns out that the telephone is actually ringing, it rings until I understand, until I hear it and register the sound. I look at the pulsing, illuminated screen, I recognize the number and my heart runs a marathon inside my chest. I make this moment of triumph last, stretching it out, enjoying it. I look through the window at the twilight on the other side of the glass.

I hear the ringing and I think that, after this call, it will be over: my years of measured boredom, of comfortable hatred, of going to sleep in the knowledge that, however much effort I exert, the world will continue on its course and that, when my death arrives, somebody will place a three-line announcement in the newspaper.

The sound, the vulgar sound of the telephone, could be the most heavenly music.

"Hello. I've been waiting for you to call."

"How did you know I was going to phone?"

"I just knew."

"Don't mention any names."

"No, I won't say your name."

"Thank you."

"Where did you get to? Tell me. I was worried."

"I can't tell you now, we can do that later."

"All right. We'll talk later. I hope you're not at home right now, because there's someone who must be searching for you everywhere."

"Don't worry, I'm not at home."

"Don't say anything if you think that's safer."

"Shall we meet soon? I'll be waiting in front of your place. In a couple of hours?"

"Today? In front of my place? Now you've called me I'm a bundle of nerves."

"It's okay, I bring good news."

"Bring it, bring everything: the house in Carrasco, the swimming pool, the luxury cars, bring the lot. The beach vacations beside a green sea, the weight-loss clinic, the Nile cruise."

"We can meet for dinner. What do you think? The Rara Avis?"

"I love it. Tonight we'll dine at the Rara Avis and drink a toast with the finest champagne."

"We'll talk and I'll apologize for disappearing for so long. I let you down, I know, but I'll tell you what happened, why I disappeared."

"There's no need to apologize. That's not how I see it. I'm sure you did what you could under the circumstances. We're not gods, we do what is within our powers. And I always trusted you. I knew you'd come back."

"You don't know how much your trust means to me."

"Our relationship is strong enough to survive any little mishaps. See you in a couple of hours. Goodbye."

"Goodbye."

"Wait, don't hang up, I need to tell you something else. I'm glad you called, not just because of the money, not just because of our friendship. Above all, I'm glad because it shows your integrity, your decisiveness. I'm glad you called, because I can't stand weak-willed people. God spits out the faint-hearted."

And we end the call.

———

I will get up, open the wooden shutters and the window to let in the cool of the early evening.

I will look at the sky, the lights in apartments and cars, the illuminated adverts, the whole city gradually lighting up, bit by bit.

In the darkness, an old, creased nightgown will billow around me in the draught.

I will breathe in the cold air, half-closing my eyes. When I shut the window I will see myself reflected in the glass, a beautiful image projected over fragments of light. I will hum a song.

How beautiful life is, even if it's only a pretence. I will smile, and run to the shower.

My shell will break. I will no longer be the person I once was.

II

This part of the story could begin with the image of a woman sitting at a desk. The woman is a captain in the Montevideo police force; her name is Leonilda Lima, she has just listened to a phone conversation, and now she can hear the empty silence that follows a goodbye, when the call is over.

She looks stern; she removes her headphones and places them on the wooden surface, fidgets with her pencil, with her notebook. She reads and rereads the notes she took while the two people were speaking.

The woman sitting at the desk is neither pretty nor ugly, neither young nor old. Everything about her is anodyne, unremarkable, apart from her hair, which reached Uruguay two hundred years ago on a slave ship and appears to have a life of its own. An expression begins to take shape on the captain's lips, her even white teeth are revealed, and we think she might be smiling.

It's after half past five in the evening in the city of Montevideo; this scene is unfolding in an office, a space barely larger than a closet. At this latitude, it is the middle of winter. The day has been chilly, grey, rainy, and night has started to fall.

117

Leonilda, we were saying, is fidgeting absent-mindedly with the pencil, with the headphones. She looks from the piece of paper in front of her to the window of her office, and to beyond the glass, and the expression forming on her lips is, without a doubt, a smile.

Until half an hour ago, she was convinced Saturn and all the other cursed planets were aligned against her; now she feels a cautious optimism which, as on so many previous occasions, may turn out to be unfounded.

But our captain is prudent even in hope. She has been waiting for this moment for many days, waiting for the phone to finally ring, for this particular person to finally call, and we can understand that she feels a discreet, careful joy, one she herself fears will be short-lived. Because this woman, Captain Leonilda Lima, is a person made of failures. And what is one failure in a life? And a hundred failures, a thousand failures? We all fail all the time; even successful people and businesses are built on the foundations of setbacks and defeats, disasters and disappointments.

Leonilda's whole life and her police career in particular have been like walking over a bed of nails, trying to climb a steep snow-covered slope, and she is beginning to tire of trying to build on the basis of difficulty and exhaustion, tired of so much hardship, tired of sacrificing so much to obtain so little, bored of always reaping the same meagre rewards.

Like everyone, Leonilda is starting to yearn for some success.

The latest setback in her police career could be titled "The Failure of the Case of the Assault on the Armoured Truck", a case to which she was assigned and from which she was then removed by her boss, Inspector Clemen, under circumstances that she, a typical blunt Capricorn, someone who respects the truth and abides by the rules, found strange. He was categorical and clear: the captain had to give up the case, and stop following the mysterious woman, Ursula López, and the suspicious lawyer, Antinucci, and stop looking into anything else that might lead her in the direction of further evidence.

Although the excuse was technically acceptable and unquestionably legal (Inspector Clemen adduced an error in the captain's assignment to the case when it had already been allocated to another colleague), she has reasons to believe she was distanced from the case so Clemen could guide the investigation into the heist. But to guide it where? She doesn't know; she tries to find out, she has some suspicions, she even has some evidence.

She looks through the window and, without being sure why, thinks about the barrio where she grew up, the place where her family made their home when they arrived in Montevideo from the north, from the department of Artigas; that neighbourhood of low houses, of bare concrete blocks. Leonilda suspects that the fact that the hold-up occurred there, in the place where she spent her childhood, is not a coincidence but is, rather, a sign, an omen even. An omen of what, though?

Our captain believes in the cosmic interplay of cause and effect knitting together the facts of our existence, creating a long chain in which each link has its own meaning, one that relates to the link that precedes it and the one that follows. Yes, an elegant, hermetic theory which, like so many elegant, hermetic theories, offers as its sole explanation the existence of a mysterious order that is, by the way, beyond our comprehension.

Leonilda tries to set aside her beliefs and return to reality, to the present, tries to give order to the facts she deems relevant. She tries to put them in a row, one after the other.

There was a terrible explosion caused by a rocket-powered grenade.

There was an assault on an armoured truck transporting money.

When she arrived, it was carnage: the vehicle was still in flames, there were shards of glass, scraps of bodywork and plastic, twisted iron, steel splinters.

Fresh blood. Charred corpses. Severed limbs.

Now the memories parade before her eyes; she tries to shut out the macabre details of the scene, focus on the relevant information, but she can't.

The wind had blown away all evidence of the disaster: the foam that filled the seats of the vehicle, scraps of imitation leather and paper and cloth, fragments of banknotes that onlookers ran to gather up, the remainder of the money destroyed by the explosion, burnt by the flames, all the cash disappearing in the fire, if we hold with the official version repeated in the press. A version she doesn't believe.

The rain, which was little more than a gentle drizzle when she got out of her car, had turned into a violent downpour, beating down on Leonilda's body as she ran, seeking to protect herself both from the water and from the horror with her hands, her arms, the collar of her coat.

The captain stopped ten yards from the burning truck; she observed the flames, her brow furrowed, her fists clenched, standing in front of the blackened remains, and finally lowered her arms, powerless to defend herself against the elements, against fate, against the atrocity of it all.

And Antinucci, the lawyer who arrived at the scene of the crime almost at the same instant as her. How should we classify him? Where should we locate him in this story?

Mara, an old woman who lives in the neighbourhood, claims to have seen him firing the weapon at the cash truck. However, dozens of people say that, when the explosion occurred, he was visiting his clients at Santiago Vázquez Prison, and that he drove past the scene of the robbery on his way back to the office, almost half an hour after the detonations.

Yes, it's true, she was there, and he approached to offer his assistance. It's also true that Mara is about a hundred years old and doesn't have all her marbles.

However, there is also the fact that, some hours later, she saw Antinucci with Ursula – the mysterious woman who lives in a building at the corner of Calle Treinta y Tres and Sarandí, the woman she has been tailing since the day of the attack, the woman she hopes will appear each morning as she sits having breakfast in the bar across the road. In vain, because so far all she has discovered is that the woman goes to therapy for fat people and that she buys packets of cookies from the Venezuelan guy who runs the grocery store round the corner. But Leonilda insists on investigating, she has a hunch and, going against her custom of obeying her superiors and following rules, she has felt driven to unravel this tangled plot in which the guilty and the innocent are not what they seem.

———

And now this happens: the police phone-tapping system has allowed her to listen to the conversation between Ursula and an unidentified man, who Ursula has arranged to meet in a couple of hours' time.

As a result, the captain is indebted to the technician who has put his job on the line by acceding to her request for a phone tap. She knows she is sticking her nose where it doesn't belong. Her sense of duty, of obedience to her superiors, is in conflict with her instincts, and she doesn't know what to do.

She taps her headphones with her pencil and thinks, as fast as she can. She has less than two hours to decide which path to take. The first option is to disobey her boss's orders, follow Ursula to the Rara Avis and risk suspension or, even worse, dismissal.

What interest does her boss, Inspector Clemen, have in this particular case? She suspects it is something personal but she doesn't have any proof, and experience dictates that it would be prudent on her part to take the second option, to do nothing. Do nothing and chalk up another failure, one more for the list. Start to die of failure, because the things that have gone wrong in the past have a habit of raining down on us, all at once, and the effect can be fatal. Gradually and then all of a sudden. We see them as if in a painting, a photo, in which all our setbacks, all our disappointments, all our defeats are gathered for a group portrait. And seeing them like that is painful and terrifying.

Her thoughts return to Ursula. What is her relationship to the man whose voice she heard on the phone? She said, "I'm glad you called, and not just because of the money." What money was she talking about? It could be any money, the world revolves around money, it could be the payment of a debt, remuneration for services rendered. She looks at her notes, neat, fast, black penstrokes: *Rara Avis. I knew you'd come back. The money* (*money* is underlined).

She repeats the final words of the conversation, the quote from the Book of Revelation, she repeats them and recognizes another mysterious sign, another coincidence. She feels the dart aimed straight at her heart, holds her head in her hands and closes her eyes, concentrates on herself, on her professional life, on her private life, on that unbounded spiral where the police captain and the woman merge, and thinks that what Ursula said to the man who called her is so very true: God spits out the faint-hearted.

III

A woman sweeps across the worn marble of the stairs of the apartment building where she lives, her hand barely touching the rail, polished smooth by so many other hands during the course of the last eighty years. She is neither athletic nor thin, she is not particularly young, and we might expect her to descend more slowly, more cautiously, to stop on each landing between the floors; we might expect to hear the sound of agitated breathing.

She comes down the stairs, in a hurry, not thinking – as she usually does – about how her excess weight could cause her to trip and lose her balance, to stumble and fall, to roll all the way down until she reaches the bottom. She doesn't think about how, if she slips, her body will plummet downwards, bouncing on the worn stairs, her head will strike the edges of the treads and the corners of the handrail, where wrought iron meets bronze. Nothing of the sort. Today, her feet are flying, carrying her without a care.

Why doesn't she use the elevator, the elegant old apparatus made of wood and brass and steel? The reason is simple. The elevator hasn't worked for a long time. It's been stuck between the first and second floors for months, and she has become accustomed to walking up and down, although usually at a far more leisurely pace than the one she deploys today.

We see her face in close-up: she is flushed, and perspiration is starting to accumulate around her open, smiling mouth. She is lightly made up, just enough to accentuate her beauty. She has taken great care over her clothes, loose black garments that suit her, even if many people, slaves to ideals of beauty imposed by some mysterious criterion, would say she is a few pounds overweight. And perhaps she is a few pounds overweight, although certainly not as many as she believes. Yes, she is a woman whose weight has cast her into an inferno from which it is difficult to escape; but today is a new day, and she is ready to tear down the gates of this hell.

Ursula descends, almost at a run, as we were saying, and reaches the bottom. She walks past the cage of the broken elevator, glances in passing at the mound of garbage that has accumulated at the bottom of the shaft during the many months in which it has been out of service: cigarette packs, chewing gum, receipts, plastic bags, cartons of wine or juice. She shakes her head and sighs, then continues before pausing in front of the mirror in the hall, looks at herself, straightens her hair, thinks of something that makes her smile. What does she think, what does she feel, what makes her appear so happy? She throws a kiss at her reflection, smooths a lock of hair, turns the handle, opens the door. A gust of wind hits her in the face.

And Ursula goes out into the street.

She leaves as if initiating a ritual, as if inaugurating a new era, smiling and undaunted, not thinking about her weight or her unpaid bills or the abandoned translation, she launches herself into the street with the enthusiasm of a pioneer, her hair dishevelled and her clothes flapping around her body, breathing in the warm air, happy and ready for anything, she goes out as if she were about to conquer the world, about to plant a flag in virgin soil. She goes out as if she had been reborn.

On the other side of the road waits Diego. He has grown a beard, with the survival instinct of animals who change their colour to deceive their prey or their predators. At first glance, Ursula doesn't recognize him; she only notices the man when he waves timidly at her. They approach. They greet, their hands reach out, then they kiss, cheek brushing cheek.

"Hi, Diego."

"How are you, Ursula?"

"I'm well. You look different. I didn't recognize you."

This meeting produces one of those moments character-ized by a degree of confusion, a certain awkwardness that both know they must make the effort to break through. They know, and they say what has to be said, meaningless small talk – the wind, the cold, the rain – they laugh for no reason, look at each other, finally they relax. He points towards the south and they walk in that direction.

The dynamic of the relationship between Ursula and Diego is strange, hard to understand and even harder to explain, so we won't waste time with pointless formulations and will instead allow the reader to judge for themselves.

As we watch them disappear down Calle Treinta y Tres, we will observe that, despite the fact that they appear unre-markable, the kind of people who wouldn't kill a fly, these two individuals were responsible for making off with the loot from holding up an armoured truck.

However, as we observe them, we cannot help seeing a man and a woman who feel a shared sympathy, having a friendly chat, side by side, strolling unhurriedly to who knows where.

IV

The Hobo opens his eyes as if waking from a nightmare.

He looks slowly around without fixing his gaze on anything, allowing it instead to slide across his surroundings, to float in the air. He seems lost. He narrows his eyes to form two slits through which the black of his pupils is barely visible.

The sunlight enters through the window and divides his body in two: one part full of hard shadows, the other part luminous with the aura of a saint. As is usually the case, neither part reflects reality.

He sees the needle stuck in his arm, between the tattoo of the skull with the gleaming eyes and the Gothic lettering spelling out the name of a rock band. The nurse holding the thermometer feels she is being watched and looks up; there is a look of alarm in her eyes, fear forces her to take a step back. Because, even supine and defenceless, even when he has just come out of a coma, there is something of the wild beast about the Hobo, something of the predator about to pounce on its prey. The woman attempts to overcome her surprise, tries to make her voice sound calm.

"And how are we feeling today, Mr Prieto?"

Ricardo moves his fingers, clenches and unclenches his fist, tries to raise his hand, lifting it a few inches before it falls heavily back to the sheet. The hand is still but tense: a beast that crouches and waits.

"Can you talk, Mr Prieto? The doctor will be here soon."

There is no response; the nurse hurries out of the room, taking a tray of syringes and gauze and pills. She leaves quickly, her white rubber clogs slapping the floor. Outside the room, she leans against the corridor wall, closes her eyes for a few seconds, lets out a sigh of relief.

These patients sent by the prison system scare her, some of them are thieves or rapists or even worse. Best not to think about it. She heard that this Prieto… no, better not to think about it, otherwise she'll never be able to go back into that room. It was so much better when he was in a coma.

Let us return to the sunlit room.

The Hobo hears noises nearby, voices, the sound of an argument that he suspects or remembers having heard before, two people talking heatedly. He recognizes Antinucci's voice before he hears the clipped sound of his Italian leather shoes on the hospital tiles, before he sees him come through the door. Antinucci stops beside the bed.

"We seem to be making a recovery."

Ricardo looks at him and then looks around, at the window, at the nightstand, then focuses on Antinucci and seems confused. Although we don't know if he is actually confused. He is, after all, a dangerous criminal and, for a man like him, feigning confusion must be as easy as robbing an old lady.

In the air is that smell that exists only in hospitals, a smell capable of hiding the stench of a sick body.

Antinucci sits on the bed, crosses his legs. He is wearing his new smile, and he displays it generously. He opens his mouth and leans down, bringing his face close to Ricardo Prieto's: the Hobo's eyes hold his gaze, two narrow slits, two dark points focused on Antinucci, inches from the lawyer's face.

"You recovered your health, Hobo. Enjoy this gift from God."

The Hobo laughs for no apparent reason; we think he is laughing at the words *enjoy* and *gift*; above all, we think he is laughing at the word *God*. That's what criminals are like, no respect for anything.

Antinucci doesn't appreciate the laughter but continues to smile, to show the implants that have cost him a fortune, thousands of dollars' worth, like having a top-of-the-range automobile embedded in his gums, he says.

"And don't get cocky with me. It's time for you to talk." His tone is gentle, almost friendly, and he takes the Hobo by the right arm, squeezing it tight. From somewhere comes the voice of a sports commentator, a TV relaying his monotonous staccato account of a match that lacks excitement, lacks goals.

"Suddenly I saw the woman, saw her take aim, I knew she was going to shoot me. Like a dog." The Hobo's voice is rasping, slurred, halting, like water from a tap that has been opened after a long time.

Even in his sleep, even when he was in a coma, the Hobo saw himself pointing the gun at that moron Diego, and out of nowhere the woman appeared, looked at him, took aim, squeezed the trigger. Why didn't he beat her to it, why didn't he shoot first? His revolver was cocked, ready to kill, and her intention was clear. Her appearance caught him by surprise, the fact that he recognized her surprised him still further. The sound of the shot still reverberates inside his skull, he feels the pain of the impact, of the bullet wound.

His ribs rise and fall, he clenches his fist – now it responds to his commands – he raises it and allows it to fall heavily on the edge of the bed, once, twice, three times. With increasing force.

"You know her?"

"Yes."

"You know who she is?"

"Yes, I know who she is."

"Tell me her name, tell me everything you know."

The Hobo's hands move towards a pocket, in search of cigarettes, then hesitate and return empty to where they were, resting on the sheet. The information is there, he thinks, he just has to recall it. He squeezes his knuckles, cracking them one by one. Crack, crack, crack. "I don't remember her name. She's the niece of Irene Salgado, the woman they said I killed, the one I didn't kill. There were two nieces, a fat one and a thin one, they were both nice-looking. I used to see them when I went to visit Mirta or to take deliveries from the store."

"If she's one of the murdered woman's nieces, her name should be in the file. They gave evidence at the trial."

Ricardo sits up, looks at him, extends his index finger. "They're called Luz and Ursula López."

The voice of the commentator can still be heard in the background, his enthusiasm and volume rising as he reports on a dangerous move which ends with the ridiculous cry of "Goooooooooooal!!!"

"Very good, very good. But no need to get upset, I'll get the information from the court records. It's a fascinating coincidence. That the woman who shot you is the niece of Irene, the person whose murder you were convicted of."

"The same. The goddamn bitch."

"And can you tell me why the woman shot you?"

"How should I know? She arrived, she looked at me, she took aim. Bang. And that was that."

"Try to remember something more, any detail that might be useful. Make an effort, Hobo."

Ricardo Prieto reconstructs the scene in his head. He sees himself pointing his gun at Diego, insulting him, holding the revolver a few inches from the man's forehead. Diego is resigned, he moves his arms like a broken doll. The Hobo presses the barrel against Diego's skin, Diego closes his eyes.

Then several things occur almost simultaneously: a woman appears on the scene, he sees her take aim and he immediately knows she is going to fire, he sees her squeeze the trigger and hears the shot, feels the pain of the bullet's impact, looks again at the woman who is holding the revolver... and recognizes her. The Hobo knows he stumbled, dropped his weapon, took a couple of steps back, staggered and looked past Diego once again. He remembers that everything went silent around him, that he crumpled, clutching his stomach with both hands. He managed to raise his head, to see the revolver with which he had just been shot, saw the hands in their surgical gloves, saw the woman holding the revolver, saw her eyes and, despite the pain spreading throughout his body, suddenly became alert, his muscles tensing.

He remembers that he looked at the woman with the gun and recognized Irene's niece. He understood or thought he understood that this was not her first crime. The pain was spreading through his chest, then he was overcome by darkness, and after that there was nothing.

"I don't have a clue. The bitch shot me, I recognized her, then I blacked out. You'll have to tell me how the story ended."

Antinucci is no longer smiling. He snorts. "This story hasn't finished yet – it's only just begun. After she shot you, the woman went off with the van, with Diego." There is a long silence before Antinucci continues. "And with the money."

"What?"

"They took the money. All of it."

"All of it? Those cocksuckers. Where did they go?"

"The Old Town. I had them followed, I think they split up in a multi-storey. I caught up with her. She still had the van but the money had gone, and then she got away too. We've looked for Diego everywhere. He's vanished, he must have left the multi-storey in another vehicle and slipped through our fingers. He's not at home. I've had the whole city searched. And not a trace of the loot."

A drop of sweat trickles down between the tattoos of blood, skulls and entrails etched onto the Hobo's chest. Ricardo Prieto's eyes are two hateful slits.

V

Leonilda has taken a decision, following a lengthy internal struggle and a splitting headache which she has more or less held at bay with a couple of painkillers and plenty of caffeine. It was a difficult decision, she only made up her mind at the last minute, and now she grabs her things from the coat stand; she is closing the office door, hurrying because she has barely enough time to reach the restaurant where Ursula López is to meet the mysterious man who was at the other end of the line. What she will do when she sees them, when she enters the restaurant and has the two of them there in front of her, she doesn't yet know. There are several paths she could choose, she thinks, various possibilities she has to consider. She takes a couple of steps and, in the corridor, hears the phone ringing on her desk. She stops, checks the time on her mobile phone, hesitates, turns back. Her sense of duty makes her open the door, go into her office and take the call just before the answering machine cuts in.

"Hello. Yes, Inspector Clemen. Of course, Inspector Clemen. I was leaving, my shift has just finished. That's all right, I'll be with you in a moment, I'm on my way." She returns to the corridor in dismay. She walks, hurrying through the maze, goes down a couple of floors, arrives at a door, knocks. From inside, someone tells her to enter. The office is spacious and well lit, an office that, unlike hers, gives onto the street, an ugly, charmless street but a street all the same.

On the desk is a thick folder with worn, grubby covers, some blank forms, a couple of ballpoint pens.

"Good evening, Inspector Clemen."

The inspector doesn't stand up, he barely raises his eyes from the papers he is leafing through, he makes a lazy gesture with his hand which could indicate boredom, impatience or be an instruction to take a seat. Leonilda thinks she observes tiredness in the shape of his mouth, an untypical lack of care in his shirt and tie, a headache in the deep furrows on his forehead.

"Captain Lima. Please sit down. Do you remember the Giménez case, the employee who embezzled millions of dollars from the bank where he worked?"

There is a hint of irritation, anger even, in her boss's voice, she thinks, but she decides to go along with him.

"Yes, I remember. But isn't the case closed? He went to prison, didn't he?"

"Exactly. He got four years. The maximum. He's serving his sentence at Santiago Vázquez. However, it seems his lawyer is going to lodge an appeal: he's turned up some new evidence. Or that's what he claims, you know how it works. So we'll have to reopen the investigation." The inspector rests his right hand on the grubby cover. "And I'm going to assign you to it."

"If you think that's best, inspector. What kind of evidence are they going to present?"

"To be honest, I don't know yet, I'm not sure what new evidence they're talking about, tomorrow I'll speak to the lawyer and then I'll bring you up to date. Is that okay, captain?" Clemen opens and closes a couple of drawers, takes out another form. Somewhere, there is the sound of a toilet flushing, a radio with a voice reading the news. Footsteps and laughter drift in from the corridor, growing gradually fainter, disappearing.

"Very good, Inspector Clemen."

"But that's not all. I have to ask you a favour. The lawyer is a friend, and he wants a copy of some documents. You'll have to go to the archive, find them, scan them. And then send them to this email address."

"No problem. I'll do it tomorrow."

"I'd really appreciate it if you could do it today. My friend is in a hurry and he's waiting for an answer. I don't think we can say no, captain." As he speaks, he pushes the folder with the worn covers across the desk towards her.

"I was on my way out and I have to —"

"Believe me, if it wasn't urgent I wouldn't ask you to do it outside of working hours."

Obviously Leonilda doesn't believe him, but she nods and agrees like any person subject to a hierarchy, because she has been subject to this hierarchy, and to many others besides, ever since she was old enough to speak.

"We have no option but to comply with this request."

The plural sounds like a mockery, like sarcasm, abuse even, and a rebellious urge makes her turn her face, looking through the window that gives onto the street, not onto a closed courtyard. She watches the buses, cars and motorbikes go by, sees people leaving their work, hurrying along. The glow of the street lights is diffused by moisture that hangs in the air, left by rain she didn't know had fallen. One couldn't say Calle San José offers a picture-postcard view, but it's still better than staring at a grey wall darkened by the passing of time.

"Here it is. Please sign here. And here. This is the address you need to send it to. Thank you very much, Captain Lima, have a good evening."

Leonilda leans forward and signs two forms. She checks the time, calculates her chances of arriving before it's too late.

The inspector is already looking at another file he has taken out of a drawer. He opens it and glances through it. She checks the time again. She leaves, then hurries along the endless corridors to her office.

VI

Let us pass over Ursula and Diego's walk to the Rara Avis, which takes a mere five minutes at a leisurely pace and during which nothing worthy of mention occurs. We can also ignore the ceremony of the arrival at an expensive restaurant, the protocol of their reception by the maître d', the way they are accompanied to their table, the ritual of withdrawing the lady's chair, offering the wine list to the gentleman and the menu to his companion; we can cast a veil over their doubts and hesitations as they choose a couple of dishes and select a bottle of wine.

We come to the moment at which the conversation has left behind questions of gastronomy, the winter weather, the comfort of their surroundings, and we arrive at the precise point when the clichés begin to subside and give way to a small silence, one that is not awkward, a silence that might even be comfortable, familiar.

And while they enjoy the pause in the conversation, we can look around. The tables are set with white linen and candles, porcelain tableware and crystal wine glasses; they are surrounded by elegant people in leather shoes, warm coats, soft knitwear, people who smile with mouths that still contain all their teeth, people who see them sitting there and suspect nothing.

———

We were saying that the clichés and the small talk had faded away to be replaced by silence, and that soon they will be able to talk calmly of their affairs, of their interests. Of their business. Yes, after a month, the day has finally arrived when our pair will address the issue at the heart of this story: the money from the heist, the money in Diego's possession.

Avarice is perhaps not the best word to describe the expression on Ursula's face as she leans forward to talk to her partner, but for now it will have to do.

They talk, exchange words and gestures. Even observing them from afar, even without knowing what they are saying, there does not appear to be conflict in the air. They seem to be reaching an agreement, a situation to their mutual satisfaction, and we see she is smiling, her shoulders have relaxed, she looks more at ease.

She is talking and appears happy, she picks up the bottle, fills the glasses, her eyes seek out those of her companion. They drink a toast. She puts the glass down gently, looks away.

Through the window of the restaurant, Ursula sees a mass of dark black clouds in the gloomy sky, and small splashes of rain appear on the panes. She is sitting down, she is comfortable. She is wearing a black silk blouse, a skirt of the same colour, made of a diaphanous fabric, and in her bag is a cardigan she knitted herself. Her legs are crossed and her hair, which is light brown, almost blonde, accompanies her movements. She seems to be searching for words or toying with the silence, until she breaks it.

"But money isn't everything, Diego."

Her eyes are bright – calm but eager – and now they are focused on a point just above the eyes of the man sitting in front of her. She flashes him a warm, persuasive smile.

"I'm going to say something, Diego, something for us to think about together. 'A man with bulging eyes.' Think, think about who I might be referring to and tell me everything you know about that man. And then we'll try to imagine how to deal with him. A brainstorming exercise. Do you understand?"

Silence. The street outside is the shade of dirty laundry, and the drizzle does nothing to improve that impression.

"I'll tell you two more things, Diego. We don't want him to find us. And we don't want him to make us hand over our money. Am I right or not, Diego?"

Diego remains silent. Outside, the wind sounds as if someone is screaming then falling silent then screaming again. Ursula observes the man's face, which wears an expression that strikes her as one of false innocence, as if he is reluctant to tell her the name she is asking for. She is annoyed by his reticence, despises his cowardice. Her anger advances, is held back, and she speaks.

"So, you've told me the money is safe. Good. Safe for now, I should add, because they could find your hiding place. So we need to think about how to stop our enemies. To stop them for good. That's why I'm going to repeat what I said. 'A man with bulging eyes.' And you can tell me who that person is."

Some disturbing memories, some submerged fears threaten to surface. Diego seems to tremble despite the warmth in the restaurant. He shakes his head.

"I'm sorry, Ursula. My mind was elsewhere."

To her, the apology sounds false, offered up as he senses

danger and tries to ward it off. Will she once again have to deal with everything?

She looks at him, assesses him, her eyes shifting from his face to his faded shirt and from the faded shirt back to his face. She waits, allowing the time and the silence to marinade.

He talks. Finally.

"It's Antinucci, the lawyer who got me out of prison. A favour he did me so I could take part in the assault on the armoured truck. But now, I don't know. He used me. He's the one who organized the robbery, the one who fired the weapon that blew up the vehicle carrying the cash." He says it and, inexplicably, he laughs, a nervous laugh, the laugh of a teenager; and, as if to reassure himself, he straightens his shirt collar. She smiles again.

"Excellent, Diego, excellent. We need to know our enemies to understand how they are going to proceed. Now, let's go to that place you know, the one where you have stored my future."

VII

As Leonilda Lima leaves her office, she wonders if the day will come when her superiors decide she deserves something better and give her an office with a window onto the street, or at least something bigger than a cupboard.

She is late, she walks past the elevator, decides to take the stairs instead, and descends two steps at a time. Outside it's very cold, and she turns up the collar of her coat. She checks the time, and when she turns onto Calle San José it is two minutes past ten. The street, which by day is full of buses and motorbikes, full of people and car horns, by night and on the corner of Carlos Quijano is a windswept desert.

Half a mile further on, after the junction with Calle Convención, the street will once again be populated by prowlers and beggars, junkies, homeless people cooking and sleeping on the sidewalk, people who pass their nights beneath the overpasses, in a part of the city that resembles Calcutta. When Leonilda reaches this part, she crosses the road to the side with the odd numbers, which is better lit or at least seems so to her. In an old building, less than a mile from Leonilda's starting point, Jack is also finishing her work and goes out at almost the same time, hesitating briefly before choosing her route and turning left onto Calle Buenos Aires.

The two women walk quickly, unaware their paths and their fates are destined to cross. Both of them sense and fear the loneliness and silence of the city; although they have never met, they are united by the unease felt by women who walk down empty streets in the darkness, united by the anxious sound of their own shoes on the paving stones.

Leonilda walks faster, she is in better condition: she goes to the gym three times a week as a requirement of her job, and she does yoga whenever she can, out of personal choice. The other one hasn't been inside a gym since she left high school. When they cross, the captain will have walked two hundred yards further than the other woman, the one she doesn't know yet but will meet in a few minutes.

We should add that Jack is a smoker and asthmatic, that she walks at a leisurely pace despite being in her early forties, and that today she is making an effort to go more quickly, to reduce the time spent between one street light and the next.

The cold and the darkness have dispersed the theatre-goers and barflies, the people who sell handicrafts in the street.

Drawing on their own experiences and intuitions, both women have that sense of anxiety in the presence of an indefinable threat, and the space between them acquires a shape, a disturbing dimension that narrows and darkens, shrinks and becomes more dense.

Leonilda, who is lean and agile, speeds up a little more, trying to keep the cold at bay. Her curly hair blows across her face, covering her eyes, and she sweeps it aside.

Now they are no more than two hundred yards apart.

Jack is alert to every shadow, her steps are heavier, she buries her hands deep in her pockets and jangles the coins against the keys. Somewhere between Alzáibar and Misiones she hears the footsteps behind her, still distant, and looks over her shoulder in the direction of the sound: she sees nothing. She regrets not having taken Calle Sarandí, like she always does when she works late; it's pedestrianized, the restaurants and bars are still open, there are more people than on Buenos Aires. The darkness seems denser in one of the doorways and she speeds up, feels her chest tightening, breathes in and out, touches the inhaler in her other pocket, turns up her collar, wraps her scarf around herself more tightly. She approaches tentatively, almost on tiptoe, but in the doorway there is nothing more suspicious than an old blanket, flapping on the ground in the wind. She sighs in relief. When she reaches Plaza Independencia, when she is safe, she will allow herself to take out the device and apply a few liberating bursts of its contents.

She hears the footsteps behind her again. The stealthy rubber soles shatter the fragile silence.

It will all happen on the corner of Buenos Aires and Bartolomé Mitre.

Leonilda, who is a little more than a hundred yards away, still hasn't seen Jack.

Jack, anxiously listening to the footsteps, still hasn't seen Leonilda.

For some people, this is just another night; for Jack and Leonilda, it will change everything. Their lives are about to collide.

Jack hears the sound behind her and tries to assume a calm expression despite her nerves, a casual air despite her unease, a mask that appears unconcerned should she find it necessary to confront the footsteps that sound ever closer, growing louder and louder. The occasional parked

144

vehicles take on a threatening appearance, the dark doorways are entrances to hell. And, without stopping, without slowing, she turns her head, looks behind her, observes, tries to penetrate the darkness.

Leonilda approaches inexorably from the opposite direction. Jack, we were saying, has looked behind her. She sees a thin man in a dark coat, sees his gleaming eyes. The man comes straight towards her, walking like a dancer trying to muffle his steps and, like her, his hands are in his pockets.

The woman turns her head and looks at him; now he is right behind her. So close. She stops. The man takes something from his pocket, something that glimmers in his right hand.

Jack has two sensations at once: she feels the gaze of his gleaming eyes, and the sting of something piercing her back. Her head still turned, she sees the gaunt face, the open pores, the mouth with a bitter grimace. And she falls to the ground.

Leonilda, less than a hundred yards away, is about to walk up the steps to the restaurant, about to enter the Rara Avis, when she sees what is happening: sees the man strike the woman in the back. She sees the confusion of bodies: one falling, the other leaning over to snatch her bag. For a moment she is astounded, immobilized. A sprinter could cover the distance in ten seconds, with forty-five strides, but our inspector is not an Olympic athlete, despite her physical training. She will run and she will take a few seconds more, and she will feel the time pass in slow motion.

As she arrives, the strap of the bag breaks, and the attacker turns and escapes with his booty. This is the point when any police officer might hesitate: to pursue the thief or to assist the victim?

For our captain, there is no question. She bends over to check the damage, takes out her phone and calls an ambulance. While she talks she observes the torn cloth, the blood flowing from the wound in the woman's shoulder, she concludes that it is not too bad and absent-mindedly strokes the hair of the woman, who is crying. She makes another call to the police.

"Don't worry. The ambulance is on its way."

"Am I badly wounded?"

"I don't think so. It looks superficial. What's your name?"

"I'm Jack, Jacqueline Daguerre. Where's my bag?"

"Jack, try not to move, stay as still as you can. Keep calm, the ambulance will be here any minute now."

"I've got the documents, the money."

"Calm down. First of all we need to make sure you're okay. We'll deal with the other stuff later."

Leonilda takes off her coat and puts it beneath the wounded woman's head, strokes her forehead, keeps her talking until the ambulance arrives.

Jack, between the tears, recognizes the face of the woman she saw following Ursula López. The face of Captain Leonilda Lima.

VIII

Ursula and Diego walk down Calle Sarandí. In the distance they see the blurry outline of Palacio Salvo in the fog; from the other side of Puerta de la Ciudadela, through the mist, it seems as remote as Australia, as Mars, as the Second World War.

They reach Plaza Independencia and pass through the gateway, cross the barren wasteland and leave behind the statue of General Artigas, flanked by palm trees. They observe the facades of the expensive office blocks where millennials launder narco cash from Mexico, Argentina and Colombia.

They go past the fountains, the concrete benches, the newspaper kiosk, and they stop right in front of the entrance to the emblematic old building. They look up, perhaps at the tower, and speak to each other. She points at something with her finger, he looks in the direction she is pointing and nods, their chins are raised, their eyes fixed on some point high up. She observes the man out of the side of her eye and asks him what he's thinking about, because you're undoubtedly thinking about something, aren't you, Diego? Don't just say anything. I can see it in your face, in your eyes.

He shakes his head and says no, Ursula, don't be so

sure, I try not to think about anything because I'm already exhausted, I want you to take over, to deal with hiding the money, to deal with the police, with Antinucci, with this whole business that has left me overwhelmed, wiped out. She nods several times, then takes him by the elbow and pushes him gently, tells him to get going, come on Diego, we've got a lot to do, take me to the place where all the money is, your future and mine. Don't worry, I'm here and I'm going to take care of everything.

It's clear that she's happy.

Somewhere in Ursula's mind are trips to Paris, weight-loss clinics and a beach with sunshine and palm trees, as there would be in the mind of anyone about to lay their hands on millions of dollars; there are houses with swimming pools and luxury cars. However, these are not the uppermost thoughts in her mind. She shakes her head, thinking.

Does she really care about the money, about the things she can buy with this money? Perhaps not. Perhaps at the beginning Ursula was hypnotized by the dream of money or the social prestige money brings, but now she is beginning to discover she wants more than that.

Yes, she's starting to suspect that what makes her happy is having won the first round of what she intuits will be a long fight for those bags of banknotes, that her success makes her happy even if it is only provisional and temporary. She hears Diego's voice but, absorbed in her own thoughts, she takes a second to understand what he's saying.

"Here are the keys to your car, Ursula. It's parked on the waterfront, down near the end of Treinta y Tres."

She returns to reality. "Great. Now we need to make sure nobody's watching us. Let's split up before we enter the building."

Diego puts on glasses, raises his hood, zips his coat all the way up. It's the first time he's been out in almost a month and he's glad he decided to grow a beard. He's also put on some weight, quite a lot.

They stealthily approach the entrance; they separate, she goes right, he goes left, each of them checking as they go.

The entrance hall of the Palacio Salvo, usually bedlam, is silent and almost deserted, apart from the night porter, who is looking at his computer, and two people walking towards the exit.

Their paths cross, they look at each other. Although his appearance has changed, somebody might recognize Diego, Ursula thinks. It's dangerous for this man to be wandering around in the building where he used to live, where the police know he used to live.

Why on earth did he rent somewhere right here?

They stop in front of the elevators, wait like two strangers, go up alone. While they are in transit, she asks him why he chose to stay here. Why did you have to rent an apartment in the same place, Diego, it doesn't seem like a great idea to have our bunker and our money right here, anybody might recognize you in the street and follow you or find out where you're staying. Why on earth did you decide to hide in the same building where you used to live?

He doesn't answer for a moment, the time the elevator takes to reach the fifth floor, the time he takes to open the door for her, after you, Ursula, to be honest I thought it was a good idea, from here I can keep an eye on my place, on my old place I should say, because I'm not going back, I can spy on the spies, I know there's been a police guard here the whole time, downstairs, in the entrance hall, and another in the corridor to my apartment, I know they left five days ago, they haven't been back since, and I was waiting for the chance to call you, Ursula, to bring you here without risking being seen, being identified, but maybe it wasn't a good idea.

She pulls a face that is impossible to interpret, gives a shrug that could be her way of saying *It doesn't matter, it's okay, Diego, don't worry, I'll take care of it, rest, you look exhausted, you're going to get ill if you carry on like this.*

They walk down endless corridors, arrive at door 511, enter the dark hallway of the apartment; and while he performs the ritual of turning keys and of putting bolts and chains in their place, Ursula looks the place over. There's not much to see.

Now her guard is down, let's look inside: she is not merely happy, she is exultant, jubilant, overflowing with this stream of heterogeneous and heterodox emotions. Ambiguous.

"You look happy, Ursula. Is it because you know you're about to get your hands on the money?"

She smiles from a corner of the gloomy living room. "I'm not sure I know exactly what I'm so happy about. I'll admit something, though: the uncertainty of adventure gives me a lot of pleasure after leading a life as predictable as mine. I feel like a different person."

"I think I understand."

"It's as if the future was saying, *come on, run, let your hair down.* Or does that sound like a shampoo ad? Anyway, you know what I mean. I don't think it's just the money. I think I'm excited by imagining what I could discover thanks to that money."

Indeed. All sorts of discoveries lie in Ursula's future, we can be sure of that.

"Now it's my turn to ask. Why do you want to run away, Diego?"

"It seems it's time for us to reveal our secrets."

"It's not a bad idea, just now, before we see our money."

"Well, after the robbery I was fleeing the police, the possibility of going to jail, all my fears. I was desperate, paralysed. But I managed to control that panic, to think, and then I rented this place as somewhere to hide myself and the money. I spent almost a month locked in this tower waiting for the damsel to come and rescue me. And when she didn't come, I rang her."

"It might sound strange, but those fears of yours, which are plain to see, surround you with an aura of vulnerability I find attractive."

"I find you attractive too. You're voracious and you don't bother trying to hide it."

"Talking of which, I'm working up quite a hunger. Show me my money, Diego. Show it to me now because I can't wait a second longer. It's in the closet, right? In the bedroom, I assume."

The apartment is small and in no time they are standing in front of the closet, which he opens with a small key on a key ring he takes out of his pocket. Inside, as he said, is the suitcase.

She looks on, still, her eyes narrowed. Ursula trembles, astonished by the orderly labyrinth of coincidences that has brought her to this place, this point in time.

"How strange, I have the exact same suitcase. Same brand, same colour."

"It's a popular model, I guess."

"I'm not so sure. Perhaps."

They are both standing in front of a closet, contemplating a suitcase they know is full of money; it's a strange moment, almost religious, and they look as if they have suddenly realized they are standing at the centre of a nuclear power plant or at the mouth of a volcano.

"How much is in there?"

"I didn't count. It weighs getting on for a hundred pounds."

"In other words?"

"If it's all hundred-dollar bills, there must be more than four million. If there are bundles with hundred-euro bills – and I think there are – then it's a bit more. And if there are some five-hundred-euro bills then it could be a lot more again."

"Don't tell me you didn't look."

"No. I just took one bundle, and I took five banknotes from that – a hundred dollars each. I lived off that for the whole month." He opens a drawer, takes out a packet of banknotes enclosed in thermo-sealed plastic. "Here's the rest."

He offers her the packet. Ursula takes it, looks at it, a miracle occurs, a transubstantiation: what in Diego's hands was money has become a chalice, some holy oil or the consecrated host itself, which she handles with reverence and returns with unction to the drawer from which it came.

She sighs, approaches the bedroom window, opens the curtain, looks down into an internal courtyard; everything seems still, dark, silent.

"Diego, we have to decide how to move this suitcase, we have to come up with somewhere safe to keep our fortune. It can't stay here. If they haven't found it so far, if they haven't tracked you down, it's only because the police are very inefficient. But it's just a question of time. Antinucci must be on our trail already. Let me think."

IX

It's a sunny, mild winter day, and that would be of no relevance were it not for the fact that Leonilda and Jack are drinking coffee at a table on the street, in the open air, in front of one of the bars on Plaza Matriz in the Old Town.

They look onto a pretty scene, like a picture postcard, one of those corners full of beauty that the city sometimes presents: the fountain with its alchemical and masonic angels, the building that once housed the colonial government, the cathedral, the Uruguay Club. But they don't see any of this; they only have eyes for each other.

Their words come and go, from mouths sometimes serious and sometimes smiling, accompanied by gestures, expressions, attitudes, until the flow stops and silence falls. We have reached that moment when there is just a gentle smile; Jack's gaze is drawn towards Leonilda, Leonilda's gaze is drawn towards Jack. If there is a shortcut that leads from words to physical caress, it involves the eyes.

The cathedral bell breaks the silence, followed by the cries of seagulls. One of them suggests they walk, the other agrees, they wander through the labyrinth of the Old Town until Montevideo begins to murmur and hum, and then the icy wind starts to blow in off the sea.

Two hours later they are at Jack's apartment, limbs entangled, their cheeks flushed, glowing with happiness. Fingers slowly intertwine, breasts press against skin. Leonilda's hair is a little messier than usual, Jack's eyeliner is smudged.

Their clothing forms a path that leads from the living room to the bedroom. Low sounds can be heard, muffled murmurs interrupted by laughter, groans, stifled cries, panting. The sounds become louder, more guttural, rising towards the end. In the chilly room there is a wave of heat, the steamy scent of their bodies.

The night will pass and dawn will come, they will be lying there, with a look of abandonment, of satisfaction, they will feel cold and will cover themselves, will cuddle up to each other, will embrace beneath the blankets.

Very early, Leonilda checks the time, she gets up and showers, she dresses slowly and without much enthusiasm.

Meanwhile, Jack heats the water to prepare some *mate*. She puts the herbs in the gourd, adds hot water and has just inserted the straw when Leonilda appears at the kitchen door. Jack offers her the brew. There is a perfect intimacy in this gesture, one hand offering and the other receiving, the fingers touching for a fraction of a second, caressing and surrounding the warmth of the *mate*.

Jack feels as if Leonilda has been there forever, it's a pleasant sensation, one that mixes familiarity with surprise.

"Did I snore?"

"Like a chainsaw."

"Oh my God, I'm sorry! I hope you managed to sleep."

"Like a log."

"What time is it?"

"Ten past six. Do you like cheese?"

"It makes me constipated."

And yes, two people who have just met, who like each other, who have slept together for the first time, also do this: between kisses, between one *mate* and the next, they discuss their bowel movements. The stuff of life.

"How's that wound?"

"Good. It's healing well. I can hardly feel it. It was superficial, luckily."

After breakfast, Jack will accompany her to the door, will knot her scarf, perhaps she will hug her tight or nibble at her lips, eliciting a kiss. Their fingers will entwine and they will find it hard to overcome their desire.

Leonilda, from the square, will turn and wave, Jack will see her expression, more serious than the one she wore five minutes ago, then she will watch Leo's back as she crosses the wide expanse of Plaza Independencia towards Avenida 18 de Julio and disappears.

Jacqueline will return to bed and clutch the other pillow, sinking her face into the smell that is already starting to fade. And so she will fall asleep, wrapped in the memory of an aroma and the image of a back receding into the distance.

X

All the wind, the rain, the fog and the cold were momentarily suspended by the arrival of an unseasonal mild spell, a series of warm days in the middle of winter. If only for a couple of days, the umbrellas, heavy coats, muddy boots and wet socks were a thing of the past. Only twenty-four hours ago, nobody could have imagined this bright sun in a clear sky, mild temperatures, the silky air which is a pleasure to breathe. Who could resist such unexpected warmth? We feel the need to go out and enjoy this time that we know will be so fleeting, this brief amnesty, to experience the somewhat artificial joy of this Indian summer.

Ursula is no exception: here she comes, down Calle Sarandí heading for Plaza Matriz, perhaps intending to sit on one of the benches surrounding the fountain with its marble angels, to feel the warmth of the sun, to breathe in the clean air.

Sebastián, the bookseller, the kid who until a month ago rented her the garage where she parked her car, approaches from the opposite direction. They see each other, stop, exchange a kiss, a hug. There is a current of sympathy or familiarity, perhaps of affection, a sentiment Ursula does not lavish on others lightly.

"Sebastián! How are you?"

"Hi, Ursula. It's been a while. Since that time you appeared in the back of the bookstore."

They both laugh. They walk side by side, around the square, looking for an empty bench in the sun. They sit down.

"If only you knew everything that had happened since then."

"A month already?"

"Almost. Nobody came to ask about me?"

"Yes. How did you guess? There was a man."

"With bulging eyes?"

"I don't know about his eyes because I didn't see him. He spoke to Fabrizio, a friend who was house-sitting. I told you I was going away, right?"

"You said you were going to be away for a whole month."

"Yes, to a spiritual retreat on a beach in the north of Brazil, no phone or anything. Well, this guy showed up when I was away, he was asking after a woman, he left a description. My friend – who has never seen you, doesn't even know you exist – told him he didn't know what woman the man was talking about."

"This person, the one asking the questions, could he have been a cop?"

"He wasn't a cop, or if he was he was in plain clothes. Some guy in a suit and tie, an executive type, Fabrizio said."

"I think I know who it is. And he hasn't been back?"

"Not so far, anyway. My friend told him I was going to be away a whole month."

"If he comes back, you know what to say, you remember what we agreed, right?"

"Don't worry."

"You're a smart lad. Thanks."

"You're welcome. I still owe you a couple of favours, Ursula. I don't forget."

"How's your brother? How's his new job at Punta Carretas Shopping?"

"He doesn't complain, because he needed the work. But being a security guard is tough, long shifts, no natural daylight. The pay isn't great, the boss always tries to cheat him out of overtime. The same old story, basically."

Ursula nods before answering. "Nico's an ambitious lad, I'm sure he'll find himself something better."

"True. And even in this dead-end job he's managed to find a bit of interest."

"Really? Something interesting in a shopping mall? That seems unlikely."

"He discovered the entrance to the tunnel that the Tupamaros used to break out back when Punta Carretas was a prison. You know the story? A passageway that joined one of the cells to a nearby house."

"Of course I know about it. Not first-hand, obviously, because I was only a year old at the time. But everyone in Uruguay knows what happened."

"So you knew Punta Carretas Shopping stood on the site of the old prison?"

"Yes. By the time they built it I was an adult. I remember it well. Tell me about this entrance. Hadn't it been bricked up?"

"Yes, it was bricked up. But because Nico is good with his hands, they asked him to patch up the plastering in the room where the security staff eat their lunch. So he started chipping away and…"

They bring their heads closer together, almost whispering. It's hot and people are in shirtsleeves, smiling, humming to themselves: in warm weather, everyone becomes gentler, their good humour spreading like a benign cloud.

Ursula seems very interested in what Sebastián is telling her, an attentive expression on her face, interrupting him now and then with questions. They take their time; neither of them appears to be in a hurry.

"I'd love to see that tunnel, it's a once in a lifetime opportunity."

"Call him and ask."

Before they take their leave, Sebastián passes her a number which she writes down in her little notebook with the pink cover.

XI

Make yourself a pot of tea, Ursula, a nice strong pot of tea. Pour it into a white porcelain teacup with pink roses and a golden rim. Add a few drops of sweetener. No, sugar is better: three or four heaped teaspoons. Put the teacup on the table beside the sofa and sit down. Drink it, without any sense of guilt. Now think. Ask yourself where your life is going.

Your money is hidden in Diego's apartment, it's safe for now. You're free, free to run, to eat or to copulate, free to buy an expensive new car or a plane ticket to Ulan Bator. Go crazy: you've got money, all your life you've wanted to have money.

But put that to one side for now, forget about the money for a second. Concentrate: there's unfinished business. You can't leave any loose ends. What happens next in your life? You know the name of the man with eyes like hard-boiled eggs, the one that made you get into his car and forced you to tell him the address of Sebastián's garage: it's Antinucci.

Think, Ursula, think: you gave him the slip the first time. You were lucky. Next time, who knows whose side luck will be on. Because there's bound to be a next time with Antinucci.

Plan: you can't leave anything to chance. He's dangerous. And when he comes, when he shows up, the day he's
waiting for you somewhere or appears in your own home,
you have to be ready to give him the reception he deserves.

Relax: allow that tense smile on your face to loosen,
allow your lips to turn up at the corners. Erase all feelings
of self-pity from your emotional spectrum.

Open the window, Ursula: it smells musty in here, it
smells old, there's too much of the past trapped between
these walls. Leave it like that, even if it blows the curtains
about. Who cares about those yellowing curtains, relics of
the past, curtains that will soon be thrown out?

Look around you: this place is like a museum. The
display cases and the objects they contain, the tapestries
from Flanders, the paintings, the threadbare rugs. Dust,
cobwebs. The rusty claw-foot bathtub, the washbasin that's
covered up. They haven't worked for ten, twenty years. Your
memories: improved, deformed, abbreviated, sweetened,
effaced. You'd like to throw out everything in this house, all
this stuff so cruelly indifferent to you, a house that doesn't
fly your flag or echo to your anthem. You were never its
queen, not even its president.

Expel the past, Ursula. Get rid of the chairs, the beds,
the tables, the mattresses. The clothes and the shoes. The
crockery and the ornaments and the paintings. Build a huge
bonfire, Ursula, and when it burns, when the flames reach
towards the sky, when the fire is burning like an inferno,
throw the 322 Japanese figurines onto it.

No, don't destroy them, keep them, look after them
until you die because they contain Daddy, they contain
your story, the one you remember, the one you don't want
to remember.

Think about Daddy. He left you everything: the fears, the prejudices, the tenderness and the violence, the shape of your nose, your blood type, your love of the Old Town and its streets, this house and the furniture, the books and the words they contain, this language and the other one that allows you to make a living from translation. He left you each of your hatreds, including the one you reserve exclusively for him.

Think about Daddy, Ursula: he is present when you choose a book in his library, when you buy the cut of meat he used to like, while you wait at the dentist's. He left you everything and he sent you off on this one-way journey, this crossing that is nothing other than the continuation of his own life.

Be angry: you can't make a pyre from the contents of this house.

Be happy: you can fill two or three dumpsters with all this garbage.

Allow yourself to go crazy: start right now, throw something out of the window. Go to the bedroom, take the chenille bedspread which looks vintage but is just old-fashioned. Tear it from the bed, roll it up, go over to the window you've opened, throw it as far as you can, watch as it unfurls, as it flies, drifts and lands down there, among the passers-by who will set their haste aside and watch the bedspread fall and then look up. The pillow with the case embroidered by Auntie Irene. Rip it open, watch the feathers fall. Shake it and throw it away too. Watch it get caught in the dark bare branches of a tree, swaying like a solitary red winter flower.

Yes, sometimes it's scary to think you might be playing at changing something that can't be changed, that this game is something you play to distract you from the insignificance of your life. But the edges of what you call your life started to blur and now you don't know what is a game and what is reality, what is your life and what is an invention. And does it even matter?

Allow yourself to be fierce; throw out something that hurts you. What about the photos? Go over to the closet, to the box full of photographs; take them out, handfuls of them, the beach holidays of your childhood with that gloomy sea, you and Luz with your buckets, one blue, one red; a trip to Rome, a snapshot of your mother with her sister; all your ancestors posed seated in their sepia lives; start tearing them up, first down the middle, then into pieces, smaller and smaller; and when you can't tear them any more, scrunch them up in your fists. Make a pile of torn, crumpled paper, throw all your yesterdays out of the window. Look how they drift, how the wind disperses them along Calle Sarandí: the pieces of Auntie Irene's face, of Mummy's hands, of Luz's blonde hair, of your eyes, the eyes of a frightened child, of the gloomy sea.

The wind whistles, ominous and terrible.

And now, do it. Do what you've always wanted. Take the blue suitcase over to the display cabinet, open the doors, sweep each shelf clear of its contents. Sweep them away, throw all those accursed Japanese figurines into the suitcase, don't spare a single one. Look at the empty display case. Doesn't the sight fill you with joy?

Calm down. Get the .38, keep it to hand. Better still, tuck it into your belt. You're at war. Don't let go of it, keep it on you at all times.

Allow yourself to be evil; think about Antinucci, feel the rage, the desire to hurt him. Be happy; he's going to suffer soon.

XII

"Let's start with Marcelo. Good afternoon, Marcelo. What do you have to share with the group today?"

"Hi everyone. Nothing much has happened this week. I mean, like always. From home to work and from work to home. I take my lunch into the office: a salad, some nuts, yogurt, a piece of fruit; three times a week I have a little chicken or ham. I don't have a problem with cravings, my colleagues are all very sensitive, none of them parades around with a slice of cheesecake smothered with *dulce de leche*, they know it would be too much for me. It's true that when I get home my mum's usually made breaded cutlets or beef stew or ravioli with cheese. Or all of them. And there's a bottle of wine on the table. And dessert. And I have to say, Mum, we've talked about this, about how I need to control my calories, how I can't eat chorizos and stews and chocolate cake. And she says, Marcelo, it's just for today. And the next day I come home and she's made beef casserole or cannelloni with bolognese sauce or tripe stew. It's really hard for me, I don't have much willpower. Obviously I don't want to be living with my mother at the age of forty-five, but like I told you, since I separated six months ago I don't have any choice. After I've handed over the money for my daughter, I don't have enough left to pay for an apartment for myself. To be honest, coming back home to live with my mum is killing me, in every sense of the word – she interferes with my life, she restricts my freedom, she's always telling me what she thinks I should do, like when I was a teenager. I've put on twenty pounds since I moved back."

"Does anyone want to say anything to Marcelo?"

(Observations, advice, opinions, general chatter.)

"Thank you, Marcelo. How are you, Susana?"

"I've had a few stressful days, maybe that was good because it helped me keep my appetite under control. No, that's not true. I didn't keep my appetite under control, it was just that with the anxiety I forgot to eat and drink. The thing is, they were making people redundant at work so everyone was wondering if they would be next. Can you imagine how stressful it is to work at a place where that's going on? I'm single, I've got two young children, their father hasn't shown up for a year and a half, he doesn't give me a single peso, he doesn't come to see them. My parents are dead, I don't have any siblings. What will happen to us if I lose my job? It's torture. My stomach is a knot and, obviously, I can't eat. Result: this week I didn't fall into temptation and I lost five pounds."

"Does anyone want to say anything to Susana?"

(Voices of encouragement, positive messages.)

"Thank you, Susana. How are you, Ursula?"

"I'm good, to be honest, really good. Since the last session a lot has happened: I got a phone call I'd been expecting for a month, and I had an important meeting. It's a kind of business deal, a joint venture with a friend, something that could change my life in all sorts of ways. Mainly financial, but there's a lot more to it than that.

And this meeting, or rather this reunion, was an incentive to stick to my diet, to keep my mouth closed and stay on the path of healthy eating: I prepared my selection of authorized food, planned my menu for each day, ate with moderation, didn't allow myself to indulge. Nothing. Apart from a couple of glasses of champagne to celebrate the reunion. And the day I went out for lunch with my sister, Luz, and the situation got the better of me. Because she hardly eats a thing, like I told you before, and generally when we go out I have a *chivito* sandwich stuffed with steak, an egg, mozzarella, tomatoes, olives and mayonnaise, and a slice of cream cake, while she nibbles at a stick of celery. That was the only exception, I only stepped off the straight and narrow with Luz. That was all. Like I was saying, this business of the company, the joint venture with my friend, was a stimulus: if I'm going to change, it has to be total. I don't want people to carry on calling me fat. I don't want that label hanging around my neck like a millstone, like a marriage vow till death do us part. I'm going to get rid of it, I've already started. And I feel proud of myself."

(Congratulations, applause, hugs.)

"Thank you, Ursula."

XIII

Perhaps he was dreaming about recovering the money from the heist when he was disturbed by the shadow of a woman who passed by his table, crossed the street and entered the building. He didn't manage to see her face, but he's sure it's Ursula. He knows it, intuits it: he has seen the eyes of this devil before.

Antinucci shakes off his lethargy, puts some money down next to his coffee cup, gets up and runs. He feels annoyed with himself for having submitted to sleep, if only briefly. But he's exhausted, he's been suffering from insomnia for almost a month, what sleep he gets is lacking in both quality and quantity, he hasn't turned up a single clue as to the whereabouts of the money. Until now, until the Hobo emerged from his coma and spoke. Since then, he's been keeping watch. He crosses Calle Treinta y Tres and heads for the building on the corner.

At the table next to the one from which Antinucci has got up, a woman in dark glasses follows him with her gaze. She watches him leave, takes a photo.

Antinucci arrives just in time to catch the door closing behind the woman who has entered the building, and he steps into the lobby to see her disappearing around the first turn of the spiral staircase. He is very tired, he thinks once again, it's almost a month since he's slept, almost a month since he's worked. He stops and waits, appreciates the aesthetic composition formed by a woman dressed in black against the white background of a marble staircase. A vision as fleeting as it is suggestive and beautiful.

He looks at the elevator, an old model with a metal cage that looks as if it's been out of order for a long time, judging by the amount of garbage that has accumulated at the bottom of the shaft. But taking the stairs is not a problem for our lawyer who, despite being well into his fifties, is in good health, eats well and takes regular exercise. Particularly now he has given up smoking, now he has managed to shake off that nasty habit.

Antinucci hears the woman's footsteps above, the soles of her shoes clicking against the hard stone, waits until she arrives at her destination on the fifth floor. He will tackle the first steps with the caution of one who knows he is in a vulnerable position should any of the neighbours appear, on their way into or out of the building, and ask him where he's going. He thinks about what would happen if that situation were to arise, if one of the residents were to surprise him as he prowls about, what he would say if they asked him which apartment he was visiting. His appearance is more than respectable, nobody would ascribe evil intentions to a man in so well-tailored a suit and such obviously Italian shoes as his. He decides to go up at a normal pace, although he tries to tread as quietly as possible. What will he do when he reaches the fifth floor? He touches the right-hand pocket of his jacket, feels the cold metal of the knife with its mother-of-pearl handle: a beautiful object, a legacy from his dear father, may his soul rest in heaven's glory. It is many years since the knife has seen service, although it was once Antinucci's youthful companion in affairs which it is best not to consider any further.

The lawyer climbs the stairs without bumping into anybody, and reaches the fifth-floor landing. He sees a solid wooden door, a classic object of the past, from the time when things were made properly, from high-quality materials, properly finished, good accessories, not like that cheap vulgar made-in-China trash, bodged together with plastic and chipboard, to be found in so many of today's homes. The lock, he observes, is a lot more modern, sophisticated, but nothing he can't open with his trusty friend.

He inserts the blade into the lock with delicacy, with skill; there is a soft, dry click and, despite his tiredness, the sound elicits a smile, it is a sound that perhaps reminds him of something, that takes him back to the good old times...

The lock is open.

He looks at the marble staircase again, listens, striving to detect any noise in the building. Everything seems peaceful. He turns the handle slowly, pushes and the door opens silently. He enters. He pulls the door shut behind him, without closing it completely, in case matters get out of hand and he has to beat a hasty retreat. Antinucci is a strategist. He knows what has to be done, what steps to take.

From where he stands he sees nobody, hears nothing. He moves silently forward until he reaches the arch connecting the hall with the room beyond.

The interior is what one would expect of an apartment in this ancient building: frozen in time, well preserved but unfashionable, the home of a comfortable middle-class family of thirty or forty years ago, which has never changed. The lawyer tends to idealize an epoch he barely experienced himself, he delights in these parquet floors made from Slavonian oak, which remind him of his home, the home of his earliest years, the panes of glass divided into panels with bevelled edges, the furniture crafted from fine wood, the decorative plaster mouldings on the ceiling. What times they were, what craftsmen the country boasted, people who came over from Europe to build beautiful houses. When you think of those modern places with their laminate floors...

He is alerted by the sound of footsteps approaching and he retreats into the shadows of the hallway; he camouflages himself against a wall on which hangs a large Gobelin tapestry, a tapestry Antinucci thinks is Flemish, judging by the bucolic scene described in silk and gold threads, peasants, sheep, a house with a pitched roof, a scene the lawyer just has time to appreciate before he disappears into the darkness. He listens and waits.

The footsteps have stopped in the next room, on the other side of the wall behind which he is concealed. There is an extended silence before he again hears the coming and going of the footsteps through the apartment, which seems very large. He hears the clatter of metal, crockery and glass, smells the scent of food cooking. It is soup, there is a smell of vegetable soup. More noise of glass, of metal, close by. Is the woman laying the dining table?

From his informants, that shower of incompetent cops under the command of Inspector Clemen, he knows that the woman lives alone and never has visitors. But it could also be that today of all days she has guests coming for lunch. To resolve any doubts, he wants to see how many dishes there are on the table, and so he takes the opportunity when the footsteps recede. He moves a few yards, peeps into the room, sees that the table has been laid;

on the tablecloth there is one bowl, one glass, one set of cutlery. He returns to his hiding place in the shadows of the Gobelin to think about how to make his entrance. His back is pressed against the wall and in his pocket his hand grasps the knife, holding tight then relaxing, and he feels a keen desire to use it again.

He hears the woman approach, perhaps with the food in a steaming dish, and wonders whether this might not be the best moment at which to appear, with the danger that the crockery will be dashed against the beautiful oak floor, his dramatic entry eclipsed by the mayhem of porcelain (French or English?) shattering on the parquet.

He hears the sound of a chair creaking slightly, cutlery clinking, sucking sounds of what he imagines is Ursula sipping soup, which he will soon discover is pumpkin. He takes five or six steps and enters the dining room.

"Hello, Ursula."

Perhaps she heard him approach, perhaps she was already aware there was a strange presence in the house, because she calmly takes her last sip, dabs her mouth dry with a napkin, places the spoon back in the soup bowl (Meissen porcelain from Germany, he is almost certain) and only then looks up.

Ursula props her elbows on the table, interlaces her fingers and rests her chin on her hands. She observes him with curiosity, making not the slightest move to get up from her chair or to shout. Daddy always said that this apartment's one defect was the lack of a door between the hallway and the dining room.

"Hello, Antinucci."

"I see you already know my name."

"I see you already know my address."

Both of them are respecting an unstated code of courtesy and distance, despite the tension of the moment. Their tone is not friendly, they don't want to seem cordial, but nor do they wish to appear vulgar or rude.

"A good friend told me about you, Ursula."

"Was he complimentary or not?"

"That doesn't matter. The only thing is that he spoke."

"I assumed your friend would speak. If he didn't die, then sooner or later he was going to speak."

"And you did everything possible to help him cross the River Styx, didn't you?"

"But your friend didn't show up for his appointment with the ferryman."

The conversation stops and is followed by a pause broken only by the noise of a distant alarm. The lawyer coughs once or twice before speaking.

"I imagine both of us have moved around quite a bit in the month since your fantastic escape."

"Which escape do you mean? I don't want to sound boastful, but so far I've got away from you twice."

"That's true, you've escaped twice. The first was when you arrived at the scene of the crime, shot Ricardo, made off with Diego in the van and took the money – my money – from the assault on the armoured truck. The second was when I wanted to get the money back, I followed you, and I asked you very nicely to return it. You took me to the garage on Calle Treinta y Tres, you tricked me and got away through a little iron door that you barred from the other side. And you disappeared. That's no way to behave."

"I know you had someone looking for me. Without any success, obviously."

Despite the circumstances, there is not yet an atmosphere of threat or fear or hostility between them; they talk like two people who know each other only vaguely and who have just met by chance.

"Aren't you going to invite me to sit down?"

Ursula signals to the chair on the other side of the table. "Be my guest."

"Thank you, Ursula."

"I'm listening, Antinucci."

"We've delayed this meeting too long, almost a month, and I'm not one for neglecting my business or putting things off, let alone leaving them unfinished. It's true that some unforeseen circumstances have created an obstacle, an impediment to this ... visit."

She pushes a lock of hair from her forehead in a practical gesture devoid of any hint of vanity, then takes a sip of water. The soup lies abandoned in the bowl in front of her, still steaming. She carefully moves it to one side, then returns to her previous position, her fingers interlaced in the air, supporting her chin. "Let's be clear. There are no unforeseen circumstances here, Antinucci: you didn't come and visit me earlier because you didn't know my identity, far less how to find me. The friend who talked to you about me is Ricardo, the Hobo, who I presume has now awoken from the coma he slipped into. He took a bullet to the stomach after carrying out the attack and perpetrating a series of murders."

"As you seem so interested in my client's health, I can confirm that the Hobo is out of danger."

"So I wasn't wrong: he told you about me."

"Yes, if you need confirmation."

"I'll carry on. The only reason you've appeared in my house today is because you've just found out where I live.

If you'd known earlier, then this 'visit', as you call it, would have taken place a month ago."

"And why is that important? I'm here now."

"It's important that you recognize your own inefficiency, Antinucci. You're so inefficient that you couldn't even find a simple person. Me."

The lawyer looks at the tablecloth, pushes his chair back, seems to be about to stand up but doesn't. "You'll appreciate that I haven't come here to argue with you about my ability to perform my work."

"And what about the abilities of your partners? The abilities of the people you recruited to hold up the armoured truck? Because it wasn't merely the quality of your own work that fell short, but the work of everyone involved in this business."

"We've already had this conversation, unless I'm mistaken."

"Of course we have, and neither the facts nor my opinion have changed. I told you the last time we spoke. You messed up your organization of the attack, so badly that you didn't even recruit enough people for an operation of that size. What's more, one of your three recruits deserted halfway through the robbery, another turned out to be a violent psychopath who was on the verge of killing everyone in the neighbourhood, and the third fainted because he had a panic attack. And meanwhile you, from your vantage point, entertained yourself by unleashing a weapon that could have destroyed half the neighbourhood."

Before speaking, the lawyer rests ten trembling fingers on the tablecloth and gives one of his horizontal smiles. "So tell me. Am I supposed to be grateful you turned up, shot one of my men, ran off with another and took over the operation, not to mention running off with the cash?"

She looks at him and shakes her head. She makes a gesture with her hand, as if shooing away an irritating insect. "What is it with men? They never want to recognize when they mess things up."

"Do I have to listen to your moralistic reflections on the failings of my sex?"

"This is my house, these are my reflections."

Ursula notices that Antinucci's eyes are red and tired. He appears to be struggling not to choke on his rage. From another apartment comes the sound of laughter, some piano chords, the voice of a singer. They both maintain the silence for almost thirty seconds.

"We need to talk about the money, Ursula."

"Let's talk."

"I could destroy your life."

"You're a bit late for that."

"Very amusing. I don't have much of a sense of humour myself, but I know how to appreciate yours. I believe I once heard someone say that humour is desperation disguised as elegance."

"I'm glad you find me elegant. Do you also think I'm desperate?"

The tension eases. For the briefest of moments it seems that he is about to smile, but he doesn't.

"Let's get back to our business: the money."

"The money."

"Ursula, you can't escape any more. I know where you live, what you do, I can use whatever methods I need to make you talk, including some not approved by the Universal Declaration of Human Rights."

The fact that Ursula remains calm in response to these words – despite the fact that she has never read and never will read a self-help book, does not do yoga, does not meditate – speaks to us not so much of her emotional balance as of her bravado, one might even say of a certain death wish. In any case, and at least on this occasion, Eros triumphs over Thanatos, and she says (with a hint of velvet in her tone): "Are you trying to frighten me? You've been successful."

"I'm glad to hear it. I detest using violence against ladies. Although if there's no other option…"

The note of vulgar, sexist arrogance in the man's voice infuriates her. Don't invent some stupid, superficial excuse: if you decide not to use violence against me it's because it would bring you more problems than benefits. Don't disappoint me, Antinucci, don't behave like an intellectual featherweight. (That's what she thinks, but she doesn't say it. However, she does respond with a touch more velvet.)

"Don't worry, you won't have to resort to violence."

"I'm glad you've seen reason. That's what I like."

Ursula sighs, unable to take any more. She can't stand his arrogance. There is no longer the slightest trace of velvet when she answers: "I hope you don't think I've decided to renounce my money."

Antinucci perceives the hardening of her tone and the change in mood this indicates. He runs his hand over his slicked-back hair, opens and closes his eyes with their excessively fleshy lids. He looks at her, sees mystery and a certain grace, and once again hates her, wants to hurt her. His horizontal smile disappears as he bites his upper lip.

"I don't need to tell you I'm armed. The knife I used to open the door."

"I heard you opening up and I knew you had come in, I guessed you were hiding in the hallway. I smelt a presence, breathed in your aroma as soon as you entered. Aftershave scented with bergamot and rosewood, unless I'm very much mistaken. But let's get back to our business, to your threats. What are you going to do? Stab me in the arm, in the leg? I think we can rule out murder, because that would mean losing your only chance of finding the money. Forever."

"I can take you far away and subject you to practices whose existence you would rather not even know of."

Ursula decides it is better to hold her peace and to wait; this is getting out of hand. She sees that Antinucci is dripping with sweat, she smells it; she identifies each note of his aroma, the mixture of bergamot and rosewood in his aftershave fuses with the scent of adrenaline and cortisol from his armpits; she smells the animal fury rising in this man sitting in front of her.

Is she afraid? She is, and right now she wishes she could put thousands of miles between her and Antinucci. But she has to be careful, clever. When she speaks, her tone is the one she used earlier, velvet with a touch of sympathy that – admittedly with some effort – she manages to pull off quite well.

"What do you propose, then? Let's talk."

"The money. All of it."

"All of it? Really, Antinucci?" The tone is one of surprise, the tolerant incredulity with which we respond to a child's nonsense.

"Enough of the silly games, Ursula." His hand moves to his jacket pocket and emerges with the knife with its mother-of-pearl handle.

"I quite agree, Antinucci. Enough of the silly games." Ursula's hand moves to her lap and emerges with the .38, which she levels at the lawyer's forehead.

The table is long and wide, big enough to seat twelve. They are sitting opposite each other; if Antinucci wanted to use his knife, he'd have to run around the table to reach his victim, and we suspect that en route he would receive not one but rather three or four bullets from a woman who could plausibly claim she had shot a stranger who had entered her house. In short, if one had to bet on a winner in this contest, even a child would know who to choose. The lawyer sizes up the situation; he puts away his knife and stands up. There is no smile on his face.

"We'll be seeing each other again very soon."

"I'll be waiting for you, just like today."

Ursula wishes Antinucci a good day. She follows him to the door without lowering the revolver, her hand perfectly steady. The departure scene is swift but slows down as he opens the door and freezes for a few seconds when he stops on the threshold and turns to look at her.

We have the impression they are measuring each other up, with a degree of disappointment, perhaps because neither of them has won or lost; it was all a brief masked ball, a scene from a play that must be repeated until, in a defining moment, there is a victor.

Antinucci leaves. She watches him descend the stairs, listens as he reaches the bottom floor; she locks and bolts the door, leans against it. How unpredictable and changeable women can be when they feel their world is threatened; and even this woman, who is capable of killing and of doing so without the least hint of dismay, holds within her another woman of a more traditional cast, one still influenced by middle-class morality.

She is pursued by a vague sentiment of guilt, but she doesn't want to think about that right now; she just wants to give expression to her fear. And she does so in the only way she knows. She cries.

XIV

Night-time. It is raining.

She looks outside and thinks about how storms can herald almost anything: they can bring cold in summer and warmth in winter, and above all they can gift us one of these evenings when the light fades slowly, flickering on the horizon. The rain is beating against the windows, teeming down onto the square, here in this part of the world. Jack enjoys listening to its indecipherable noise and contemplates it in rapt attention, not moving from the window. The downpour only lasts five minutes; the rain and the storm head south and, just as quickly, the dense, vigorous odour of earth, of clean air, reaches Jack where she stands by the window. She breathes deeply, inhaling the glorious smell before it dissipates, before it evaporates with the wind. The square is deserted, she thinks, but she realizes she is mistaken, a man has appeared from a doorway, from some provisional refuge against the storm; the man settles himself to sleep on a bench without even taking the trouble to dry it, without making any preparations other than rolling up what appears to be a bundle of rags and resting his head on it. Leonilda hurries across the square, the water streaming off her. Jack sees her coming and runs to turn on the oven, waits for her to come up, they embrace at the door.

"I've made beef with…"

The sentence goes unfinished; deprived of meaning, it floats in front of the door as it closes, drifts down the corridor, zigzags in the window of the bedroom that looks onto the square, hovers above the bed, then dissolves and is forgotten.

The hour passes, the hands racing round the dial of the kitchen clock. Jack and Leonilda get dressed, lay the table and sit down to eat.

There they sit, facing each other, eating roast beef with potatoes. They are in the midst of the ritual of discovering each other, of understanding each other.

"How was your day, Leo?"

"Busy, and I had to do everything twice: I've had things to do inside the police office and outside as well."

"Why inside and out? I thought you worked in an office. You told me you were a captain. You don't have to go out on the beat, do you?"

"No, I don't go out on the beat, but I'm doing an investigation … on my own initiative."

Jack feels her shoulders tighten. She hasn't yet told her that she recognized her the first time they met, that she knows what she's talking about, that they're both tailing the same woman. She decides it's better to say nothing for now, to wait until they have established a relationship of trust.

"A private investigation? It must be something important."

"I can't tell you much, it's classified for now. All I can say is that I'm following a woman, here in the Old Town, and that I suspect her of having been involved in something big."

"Really? Something big?"

"I can't say anything more, Jack. It's classified. Confidential. Anyway, how was your day?"

Jack's cheeks are flushed and her eyes are shining; she furrows her brow in an imperceptible expression of annoyance or surprise. Ursula is involved in something important? Leo must be wrong, they can't be talking about the same woman. Yes, there must be a mistake.

"How was my day? It was routine, boring. I also followed a woman in the Old Town, but there's nothing interesting about her: a woman who only goes out to buy food, to go to therapy, and that's about it."

"So why are you following her? Who's paying you?"

"Her sister. She's got it into her head that the woman's up to something."

"What's she supposed to have done?"

"Anything and everything. Driving about in the countryside at night. Believing their father committed suicide by taking an overdose. Having a ring that had been stolen from their aunt. Who knows."

"The sister who hired you to do the investigation suspects her of everything and nothing?"

"Exactly. So off goes Jacqueline, following the woman all over the place, submitting a daily report that says she went to a meeting for compulsive eaters or bought two pounds of potatoes in the store round the corner."

"It doesn't seem a lot to suspect the poor woman for."

"If someone pays me to follow somebody, I don't argue. In the end, something came up. It's not much, but —"

"What was it?"

Jack looks through the window. A melancholy peace has descended from the sky above the square. The thoughts crowd inside her brain; she considers the words she is about to utter, measures and weighs them, asks herself if she shouldn't have said something before, makes up her mind and speaks. "The woman I'm following spent almost a month locked up at home, she barely went out in all that time. Then one day she met a man, and they went to the Rara Avis. It's not much, but —"

"The Rara Avis?"

"Yes."

"And she lives in the Old Town, you said?"

"Yes." She observes Leonilda, her hair tousled and still wet, her hair gleaming bronze in the lamplight, and thinks she detects surprise in the furrowed brows, the line of her forehead.

"What's this woman called, Jack?"

"Ursula."

"Ursula López?"

"Yes. That's her."

A look of surprise, of relief, appears on their faces. They are both silent, each lost in their own thoughts. Jack thinks about the word *coincidence* and Leo thinks about the word *coincidence*. One of them is thinking that there is no logic to any of this; the other is thinking that there is a hidden logic to everything, even if we can't see it.

They raise their heads at the same time, they don't know what to say. Jack stares at a piece of bread she is rolling between her fingers.

"I think we need to talk about our woman, Leo."

"I think you're right."

"It doesn't make any sense for us to carry on being so reserved: we're after the same person. And there's more: I've known it since the start, since I saw you."

Leonilda struggles to control her shock, perhaps also to overcome certain prejudices of an ethical nature, and this struggle also contains a large dose of injured pride, of trust betrayed. "You knew? You always knew?"

"I always knew. When I was watching her I realized you were watching her too. What I didn't know, and I still don't, is why."

Leonilda sighs. She takes the decision to speak. "I think she's involved in the robbery of the armoured truck."

Jack bursts out laughing. "That can't be right. We can't be talking about the same woman. You're saying Ursula López was involved in the cash truck robbery? You're winding me up."

"I think she was involved, but I don't have any evidence yet. The only way to prove it would be to find her with the stolen money. This salad is delicious, Jack. What's in it?"

"Fennel."

Leonilda feels like she should be angry, like she ought to demand explanations. But Jack looks so pretty, like a fairy, like a fragile, delicate spirit, a being who has come from another, more beautiful world. A wave of fierce, vibrant tenderness surges through her veins, and the flickering flames of her desire threaten to rekindle. She caresses the hand that lies on the table. She wants to place her trust in this person and thinks that sometimes this is how trust is born, as a deliberate act of honesty, of familiarity, of loyalty towards someone who, by the light of the candles, looks as exquisite as Jacqueline.

XV

Dawn is breaking in this part of the world and, although the forecast is for sunshine, at seven o'clock the rain starts to fall so hard that it feels as if someone is throwing sharp nails down from the clouds. Seen from above, the city seems more anarchic, there seem to be more cars, more buses, more car horns honking, more people walking around armed with umbrellas and stepping in puddles, tripping on cardboard boxes and bags full of garbage and loose paving stones. When it hits the city, the rain imposes a paradigm of chaos in a place that is already chaotic and dirty and which then becomes a little more so. The downpour is brief and heralds an electric storm full of dramatic phenomena, of cumulonimbus, of lightning, of explosive sound effects, a storm that soon heads for the north of the country. The calm arrives, the clouds disperse above the city, once again shafts of sunlight appear and the air is cleansed of dust, as if brand new. A pure new light spills over the streets.

Antinucci receives from heaven what he had asked of it: a beautiful sunny day, a clear, mild, beautiful winter morning, the temperature almost springlike. We wonder why Antinucci is so interested in the weather, but we won't know the answer for a while, until he reaches his destination.

For now, we must be content with the knowledge that he is driving east along the Montevideo shoreline in his Audi A6 Allroad Quattro, the Bullet that, according to its owner, is worth every cent it cost. He sighs with satisfaction; it is a sophisticated machine, with cutting-edge mechanics, with walnut detailing on the doors, steering wheel and dashboard, chrome metal, seats upholstered with the most expensive leather. This man is obsessed with leather. The upholstery in his car, the folders in which he keeps his documents, the chairs in his office; all the important objects in his life are covered with leather of the highest quality, and this extends to his collection of Italian shoes, more than fifty pairs painstakingly organized by colour.

He removes an imaginary speck of dust from the blue screen on the dashboard.

As always, he is listening to music, in this case the first choral part of Bach's *St Matthew Passion*. He hums along, quietly.

> *Kommt, ihr Töchter, helft mir klagen,*
> *Sehet! Wen? Den Bräutigam.*
> *Seht ihn! Wie? Als wie ein Lamm.*
> *Sehet! Was? Seht die Geduld.*
> *Seht! Wohin? Auf unsre Schuld.*
> *Sehet ihn aus Lieb und Huld.*
> *Holz zum Kreuze selber tragen.*

Two fingers tap out the rhythm on the steering wheel. When he listens to music and feels at peace, there is an expression of beatitude on his face, and we can imagine him practising the law in a comfortable office with green walls, or mowing the lawn in a vacation home on the coast.

The discordant note is struck by the scar on his forehead which, although it could have been caused by an unruly branch or the edge of a piece of furniture, we suspect was made by a fist. Perhaps his eyes are his most disturbing feature, too large, bulging, with their excessively fleshy lids, almost always hidden by his Ray-Bans, which he says he wears because he suffers from photosensitivity.

In the glove compartment is a packet of cigarettes he has not touched for a week, and that makes him feel satisfied. The acupuncture needles are still there behind his ear and his withdrawal symptoms disappeared some days ago. He had tried a hundred different ways of giving up smoking, and had failed time and time again, always returning to that filthy habit that left him full of guilt, stinking and with stains on his teeth. But this time he thinks he's about to succeed, and the thought fills him with satisfaction.

He drives east along the waterfront road. Every now and then he touches the rosary of mother-of-pearl beads and says a quick prayer to Our Lord or to the Virgin Mary or to the Sacred Heart of Jesus, something short and full of burning passion for the recipient. A psalm. *The Lord is my shepherd; I shall not want.* And indeed we could say he wants for nothing, particularly since he gained control over the traffic in cocaine and coca paste in the north and northeast of the city. He can't complain; business is booming, his profits have grown exponentially. He's always been a successful man, thanks to the Lord and to the Virgin Mary.

He maketh me to lie down in green pastures.

He still recites Psalm 23, somewhat obsessively, perhaps because he has begun to suspect that, despite the rapid growth of his business and the money he earns from it, he does indeed want for something, there is something his shepherd does not provide. He begins to doubt whether things are going as well as he believed. And all because of that woman, Ursula, who burst into his life and robbed him of his money, his peace and, above all, his self-esteem. He thinks about her, about what he is starting to call the Ursula effect, and the thought has somewhat bitter undertones.

He leadeth me beside still waters.

Antinucci grasps the steering wheel, indignant, with a desire for justice, his Audi A6 hurtling towards Carrasco, the exclusive neighbourhood on Montevideo's eastern edge. The purr of the engine soothes his soul.

He checks the time. It's 7.15 in the morning. He is a few minutes from his destination and has all the time in the world; despite this, he accelerates, he likes to put the Bullet through its paces along the waterfront at this time of day, see the beaches fly past one after another, look at the river that resembles the sea. He is travelling at speed, and the almost imperceptible sound of the engine wards off his negative thoughts. He isn't worried about being fined for speeding, that sort of thing isn't a problem for a man with his political connections.

His mood rises and falls. He squeezes the steering wheel and thinks once again about the Ursula effect, about the disorder into which his life has descended, the confusion of the past month.

He turns up the volume on the sound system and tries to concentrate on the pleasure of the music.

He restoreth my soul: he leadeth me in the path of righteousness.

But Ursula has deprived him even of this happiness, and he can't help feeling a tremor of hatred.

———

When he reaches Avenida Bolivia, he indicates left, waits for the lights to change, turns, drives two hundred yards and turns again before coming to a halt in a silent street of imposing houses surrounded by trees. He listens to the engine shutting down and checks his watch, a Flieger Type A that belonged to his maternal grandfather, a Luftwaffe pilot who somehow ended up here in the Pampas.

Antinucci looks at the perimeter wall painstakingly covered by climbing plants, designed by a landscape gardener, a wall that surrounds a garden that surrounds a mansion. He turns down the volume of the music, checks the time again, settles back in his first-class aircraft seat, feels the satisfaction of enjoying the luxury and comfort of the car. If the morning is sunny, if it doesn't rain, she will come out for a run at 7.30 on the dot.

Yea, though I walk through the valley of the shadow of death, I will fear no evil.

Antinucci watches the gate open, sees her come out; without hesitating, the woman gathers her hair in a ponytail and walks towards him. The lawyer removes an object from his pocket and opens the car door, intercepts the woman and places something over her nose. He holds it tight.

Luz resists for a few moments; she is strong and physically fit, and the man has to use all his strength to overcome her. He presses the cloth against her face until she weakens, staggers and falls to the ground, close to the car.

Antinucci bundles her into the front passenger seat, looks around, checks nobody has seen them. They promised him the effect would last for at least twenty minutes, and that's how long he has before the woman regains consciousness. He feels the passing temptation to light a cigarette, as a reward for the success of the operation. He shakes his head, makes himself comfortable, turns up the volume of the music. He fishes a pair of handcuffs from beneath his seat, takes the woman's limp hands in his own, closes the mechanism around her wrists. Then he takes out some tape, seals her mouth and her eyes, and also thinks about securing her ankles but dismisses the idea; it would be the kind of excess typical of someone who has watched too many movies. The tinted, reflective windows of the car will act as a barrier, ensuring the success of the kidnapping. Kidnapping. It makes it sound like something terrible, something sinful.

He touches his fingertips against the mother-of-pearl rosary that hangs from the mirror, bows his head and murmurs. Antinucci is grateful.

His lips tighten and he turns the volume up still higher. Then he starts the engine and drives away.

XVI

Ursula enters Punta Carretas Shopping, a mall built on the site of what was once a prison, perhaps one of the most notorious in South America, its fame due to its two most celebrated breakouts: the flight of eleven anarchists in 1931 and that of a hundred and eleven Tupamaros in 1971.

The mall occupies four blocks, is three storeys high, and below ground level there are parking garages and services. It has numerous entrance points, some of which connect the mall directly to the outside world, others via stores with access to the street.

Ursula is on Level 0. She walks along, looking around her as she goes.

She is slightly overweight, at the midpoint in her life, dressed somewhat untidily yet in a way that, far from seeming vulgar or neglectful, is suggestive of an interesting personality. A mane of light brown hair comes down to her shoulders and, when she moves, accompanies her as if in a shampoo advert. Well, perhaps that is an exaggeration, but her hair is pretty and provides a luminous frame for her face.

Ursula observes her surroundings. We don't think she is here with the intention of shopping, because she isn't looking at window displays or going into stores, she just walks.

What is she doing? Is she counting her steps? That's the impression she gives, as if she was measuring the distance between various points. She traces the path from one point to the next, lost in her calculations, stops to take a pink notebook from her pink handbag, makes notes.

A group of teenagers, perhaps on a school trip, approach from the opposite direction, stopping in front of every store, every window display, talking and shouting, touching each other, hitting each other, laughing at the slightest excuse. The boy who is in her path is your typical fat adolescent, with acne, glasses, a T-shirt with the name of a cumbia group on it. Ursula is concentrating and doesn't see him; they collide, she loses her balance, drops the book, her pen rolls away.

"Watch where you're going." Ursula looks at them, demanding an apology with her eyes. The kids laugh, shout things to each other. Finally, they pick up her notebook and pen and hand them to her. "Sorry, sorry."

Ursula's gaze could stop a herd of buffalo – or ten high-spirited teenagers. She starts walking again, back and forth: walking, counting, writing, she moves in accordance with an unknown plan. She explores the space methodically, and the geometry of movement appears to please her; she has a satisfied air. She pays attention to the sounds, looks to see where the cameras are located, the loudspeakers. She notes down everything. She takes the escalator to Level 1, takes two or three photos with her phone. She puts the notebook and the phone in her bag, searches for something, finds it a few yards away, approaches with a happy expression.

The guard sees her coming, smiles at her. Ursula knows he can't talk while he's on duty; however, they pass by each other and exchange a few words, just what is strictly necessary.

"It's all ready, like I told you. You remember how to open it?"

"Perfectly. I'm on my way."

"Don't worry. At this time of day there's nobody there."

"Thanks, Nico. I'll call you afterwards."

"Good to see you, Ursula."

She goes back down to Level 0.

The music is louder and the buzzing of the crowd soon becomes confusing, disorientating and, perhaps because of this, Ursula stops, looks around, appears irritated. It is clear from her face: she finds it hard to stand the noise of the mall, she isn't used to such places and has no intention of becoming accustomed to them.

We wonder why she doesn't leave if she feels uncomfortable, if she has already finished what she was doing, whatever that may be. We think we detect a slight hesitation in her movements, a wavering. Yes, she hesitates, then makes for the service area. She looks as if she is going to the toilet; however, she walks past the door that says LADIES and continues until she reaches another door, one bearing a notice that reads NO ENTRANCE: STAFF ONLY. She pushes, goes inside, disappears. We don't know what happens on the other side.

Some ten or fifteen minutes later, we see her emerge through the same doorway, her expression that of somebody who is satisfied or even happy with what they have done.

She won't enter stores or look at window displays, won't stop to take notes. She will head decisively towards one of the exits, go outside and walk away from the mall, continuing for another couple of hundred yards until she reaches the bus stop.

Half an hour later she is back in the Old Town, sitting lost in thought until she is distracted by a siren or an alarm or voices louder than normal. She looks up, initially with surprise: at the corner some fifty yards away, she sees four police officers, two patrol cars, an ambulance, two people in white coats who look like doctors, and a dead body. The deceased is lying on the ground and she can't see anything, the body is completely covered by a sheet of black plastic, but somehow she knows it is a dead person.

As she approaches, a brown shoe poking out from underneath confirms her suspicions.

Ursula walks towards the corner, sees that the dead body is cordoned off: two orange cones, haphazardly connected by yellow tape, separate it from the world. Of the four police officers, one is a woman, thin, very young, and she appears to be unhappy with the situation, unhappy at having to stand next to the deceased.

People walk past without realizing there is a dead person there; the orange cones, the tape and the vulgar black plastic sheet make the shape seem like a pile of rubble, perhaps the product of some repair to the street or to the paving stones. And it could be, were it not for the brown shoe. However, Ursula thinks, the passers-by don't notice the shoe because they are absorbed by the task of tapping text into their phones or waiting distractedly for a reply.

She shakes her head, bites her lip. She slows down, observes.

The ambulance and the doctors leave, so do the patrol cars; of the four police officers, only the thin woman remains. Her uniform is too big for her. They leave her on duty, looking after the dead body. She waves to her colleagues as they leave; once everyone has gone, she turns her back on the deceased or on the black plastic sheet or on the brown shoe. The officer stands watch from as far away as possible, without looking at her charge, because, after all, who is going to steal a dead body, let alone one hidden under a piece of plastic?

Ursula passes close to the cones and the yellow tape; she stops and looks but can't feel anything for this invisible dead person. It is almost as if she were indeed passing by a pile of rubble, despite the brown shoe that she now sees is old and worn. She breathes in and smells alcohol, stew, poverty. She smells the misery. She makes an effort to think about this little mound as what it is, someone who has just died, though she can't manage it: no doubt due to the black plastic that covers him or the cones and the tape that separate him from the passers-by, from the living, reducing him to something with the appearance of a pile of stones and earth. Ursula sees that the police officer is still keeping her distance and has her back turned, and she makes a decision; she steps over the barrier, gets out her phone and takes a selfie with the worn brown shoe poking out from beneath the plastic sheet.

Sometimes she has the feeling something wonderful and absurd is about to happen, something crazy, a brush with death.

XVII

Behind Ursula is the dry sound of leaves being trampled, the crack of branches breaking. There is an old scent, almost gone, of tobacco and nicotine, notes of bergamot and rosewood, mixed with leather. She sniffs, hears the voice, doesn't turn around.

"I'm going to be blunt, Ursula. You're in no position to ask for anything. As you know, I have your sister. Thankfully she's in good health, but let's hope she stays that way. I did have to smack her about a bit, nothing too serious though, nothing that will spoil her good looks."

Ursula feels a violent impulse. She bites her upper lip, understands her sister's life is hanging by the thread of her ingenuity. Even though she knows he can't see her, she nods. She is unaware of the tears that are beginning to slide down her cheeks.

"Tell me what you want."

"The money. You know perfectly well that I want all the money."

"All of it?"

"The time for negotiating is past. I'm the one setting the conditions now."

Ursula feels like arguing. But she immediately realizes this is no time for such things. She turns around to face him. "Okay. Where and how?"

As she says it she notices a movement some twenty yards away, a woman walking, who stops to light a cigarette, who is wearing sunglasses and seems to be enjoying the mild weather. Ursula has seen her several times before. Her and the other one, they seem to be taking turns to spy on her. She forces herself to push the issue aside, listens to the man.

"It could be in a park like this."

She knows what to say. "No, a park is too big, too open, too few people in winter, too spread out. I'd prefer somewhere public with a lot of people. And enclosed. I'm sure you understand that it's my insurance policy. The presence of a lot of people is the only guarantee I have that you will keep your side of the bargain and release Luz."

He snorts, clears his throat, the silence continues. "Knowing you, I assume you've already thought of somewhere, Ursula. Is it all right if I call you Ursula, despite everything?"

The woman nods, gives him a smile that could even seem friendly. She has to be careful, skilful, lead him on slowly. "Why don't you suggest somewhere, Antinucci? All I'm saying is that it needs to be somewhere large, with a lot of people, somewhere public where nobody will take any notice of us. And, as I explained, that will be my guarantee in case you don't keep your part of the bargain, in case you don't release my sister."

Another silence, this time longer. She continues.

"I'll do whatever you say. I don't want anything to happen to my sister and I don't want the police to catch me with the stolen money. I'm clear about two things: I don't want Luz to die, and I don't want to end up in prison."

Ursula knows this is her only chance. She measures her words carefully, trying to ensure – like an actress – that it doesn't sound rehearsed, artificial, even though it is. She practised her lines last night, whispering them as she lay in bed, as she took a shower, while she sat at the kitchen table, honing each sentence so as to give an impression of spontaneity today.

"It also needs to be somewhere with plenty of space, where we can walk without calling attention to ourselves. I'll need to bring a large suitcase. I couldn't exactly wander around a park or a dangerous neighbourhood with a suitcase, could I? You know what it's like. I've been mugged before. It needs to be somewhere large, with lots of people, under cover if possible, in case it rains."

"It could be a shopping mall."

Ursula hears Antinucci's self-satisfied voice and feels like kissing him. She hides her delight behind a neutral mask. "Well, maybe. I'd have to think about it. But now you've suggested it, maybe Punta Carretas would work, with that big central atrium."

"I was thinking about Montevideo Shopping."

Ursula, a woman who knows how to wait until the wind changes, doesn't give up so easily. She closes her mouth, careful not to give voice to her disappointment, and when she thinks the time has come to break the silence, she does so. "Whatever you think, Antinucci. You're in charge."

Our lawyer, who for once is not hiding behind his Ray-Bans, has the serious expression of someone who is considering a novel idea. He reflects, a few seconds pass, Ursula holds her breath.

"Although maybe Punta Carretas is better. Like you say, it's got that big central atrium. I'll be able to keep better track of your movements, Ursula. And you can make sure I release your sister."

At certain moments, when the light and the situation favour her, when Ursula forgets her defensive guard against people's judgements, she can be a very attractive woman; we might even say she shines, that she radiates a luminosity akin to beauty. And as she stands there talking to the lawyer, we see her and think this is one of those moments when she looks radiant from the combined effect of the sunshine and the success that she feels is once again within her grasp.

"Punta Carretas it is then." Ursula plays her final card: "Is three in the afternoon okay for you?"

"I can't see why not."

Standing there in Villa Biarritz Park, under a tree, like two friends or lovers who have interrupted their walk, they carry on talking for a few more minutes. There's a lot to organize: they negotiate details, stipulate the mechanics of exchanging the money for Luz. Everything is agreed in principle.

"I'm going to give you some free advice: don't do anything stupid, and don't try to trick me. Your sister will be in my men's sights the whole time, there will be snipers trained on every exit and they won't hesitate to shoot if you get up to anything suspicious. If you try to pull a fast one, I assure you that neither you nor Luz will leave the shopping mall alive."

Ursula understands two things: that she must be very careful because her sister's life is at risk, and that a new world is waiting for her just around the corner. If everything works out as planned. She inspects the expensive shoes and the tailored suit, catches the faintest hint of nicotine. And the woman in dark glasses who is standing a little way off.

"And I'm going to give you some free advice in return: stay off the cigarettes. Because you still stink. And I can't imagine it's good for a mafioso to be preceded by the smell of stale tobacco."

We don't know if Antinucci is astonished or confused.

"You're crazy."

"The streets of Montevideo are full of crazy people, Antinucci. Or haven't you noticed yet?"

XVIII

I make myself some breakfast with what I have. I boil an egg, put a slice of bread in the toaster: I've been stuck between these four walls for a month. I don't have shackles on my ankles or handcuffs on my wrists, but it's as if I had an iron ball tied to my neck with a chain that stops me from going beyond the door, that confines me to this tiny apartment with views to an internal courtyard, looking out on mouldy walls that never see the sun, the windows of neighbours who never show their faces, a scrap of sky the size of a handkerchief.

I've worked out a prison exercise routine, a combination of strength and aerobics I don't always have the willpower to complete because the confinement and lack of contact with the world have left me with a kind of paralysis, and sometimes the terror returns. The terror of the other prison, the real one, the one where I was locked up until recently.

I should call the store to order some more food. I'm almost out of bread, I need some meat, some cheese, some lentils; but I have no energy left, my tank is empty and I only get out of bed to sit in front of the TV and watch whatever garbage is on so long as it makes me forget the captivity, the loneliness and the fear.

I sit down to eat the toast and the egg, some leftovers of last night's *farinata*, black coffee because the milk has gone off.

A few days ago I checked that the police were no longer watching my house. I don't know if the three agents who were taking turns got bored or if they went off on their winter vacation; whatever the reason, they haven't returned yet.

I waited for three days to go by with no sign of them, then I called Ursula and even went to eat with her at the Rara Avis. After that, we came back here and I showed her where the money was. She said we'd need to find somewhere safer, that she'd take care of it.

I've had to spend a month cooped up in here to realize what it is I really want – and what it is I don't want.

I add three spoonfuls of sugar to the coffee and bite into the egg, which is just how I like it, soft-boiled. The gas cylinder in the kitchen could run out at any moment. I wish I had some jam, an apple, I wish I could go out into the sunlight and walk wherever I want, go back into the Palacio Salvo without looking all around me and over my shoulder, go anywhere with the tranquillity of innocence.

I can't take much more of this, I think I know what I have to do. Ursula told me she was going to call, that she would come over, and since yesterday I've been waiting for that moment so I can start planning what I need to do. She can take the money and I'll work out how to get rid of this anxiety that doesn't let me breathe.

And a few minutes ago she called to say she was coming over, she told me to wait for her. To wait for her? I never go out, I'm stuck in this dark apartment with a view of grimy walls and closed windows, alone and with nobody to talk to. Except for that one time, with Ursula at the Rara Avis. I enjoyed it, we talked, we ate, we drank, we toasted our reunion. I'd been locked away for days on end, I was going mad. I am going mad.

I have to wash and shave, to get this filth off me and put on clean clothes. What's she going to think if she sees me in this state?

I have a banana, some leftover egg and spinach tart, some sour milk, and a few million dollars in the suitcase in the bedroom closet. To think I spent years chasing after enough money to solve my problems, to get rid of the depression and the fear, and now this: I'm walled up in here with a load of money I can't spend on anything except for some apples at the store.

I'm going mad, I have to do something. Today.

I must wash my cup and my plate, take a shower.

If only I'd rented an apartment with a street view, if I could at least look out onto something other than a dirty grey wall and some windows that are sealed shut; if I could see people, if only from a distance, and the sky or something more than that patch of sky the size of a handkerchief; but I wasn't thinking. I can't go on like this, I can't take any more.

What use are all these millions, all these meaningless pieces of paper, if I can't even follow an exercise routine, can't get out of bed; or if I do, it's just to sit hypnotized in front of the TV screen?

Sometimes I think about Barcelona and the life I left behind.

Why? Why? To end up in a kidnapping, a robbery, surrounded by death? It wasn't my intention, it wasn't my intention, it wasn't... Yes, I'm a coward, and I wonder if it was my destiny, if it's genetic or if the circumstances of my life made me like that. Can you stop being a coward? Or is it a fate one can't avoid?

Though I want to wash myself, to shave, to get out of these dirty clothes, I can't even get out of this chair; all I do is think about how I can't go on like this because I'm going mad. I'm not chained or handcuffed, I'm not in an actual prison; but I feel that iron ball tied to my neck with a chain that stops me from going beyond the door, that confines me within the four walls of this apartment.

If I don't decide, I'll go crazy.

I make an effort and stand up, drag myself to the bathroom, take a shower, shave, change my clothes. When I come out, the bell goes. I make sure it's her, press my eye to the peephole. What a relief. I unlock the door, remove the chain, slide the bolt. "Finally, Ursula."

She fixes me with a stare. Then looks around. "You're in a sorry state. This place, Diego…"

"Yes, this place… You've no idea, I'm going crazy."

"Anyone would. This room, that window with its depressing view. And that picture: an apple at sunset. Jesus Christ! Do people choose to live here?"

"Promise me you're going to hide our money today."

"Don't worry, Diego, I'll take care of everything."

"Today, Ursula?"

"Right now. Relax. I've got it all planned out."

We go over to the closet, open the door with a key I take from my trouser pocket.

"It's all yours."

"Help yourself to what you need before I take the rest."

"I've got what I need, a bundle of a hundred thousand in the drawer."

"Okay. And what are you going to do? Where are you going to go, Diego?"

"I don't know, I don't know what I'm going to do. I'm tired, depressed, desperate. I wish I could get away from here until this is all over, until they've forgotten about us. But I don't know if I have enough strength left. I can't take any more. I want to put an end to it all."

"Do you want some advice?"

"Of course."

"Put that bundle of notes and a change of clothes in a bag, go to the border, cross on foot, without going through passport control, then catch a bus at the station on the Brazilian side: to a beach, to the island of Florianópolis, to São Paulo or to Rio de Janeiro. Anywhere where there are lots of people and nobody will notice you. Rent somewhere, like you rented this place. But try to find somewhere less depressing: a pretty little house, an apartment with sea views. You can afford it."

"And if they ask for documents? I have my passport. Do you think I'll have problems?"

"I'm sure there's no international arrest warrant. Didn't you see the news? The official version is that the perpetrators died in the explosion and all the money was destroyed in the fire. The only problem is Antinucci, but it's better if I don't tell you about that, it'll only worry you. Anyway, that's a problem I can solve on my own."

"Are you sure you can do it on your own? I'm in no state to help you."

"Listen to me: leave tonight. Right now. Make a fresh start two thousand miles away."

"And what about you?"

"I'm going to take this suitcase, and I'll hide our money.

Where nobody can find it, I promise. After that, we'll see. Maybe we'll be able to meet up soon and celebrate our victory. Good luck, Diego."

Ursula kisses me on the cheek and heads off with the blue suitcase as if it were a shopping cart. I watch her through the peephole, then hear the sounds of her footsteps and the wheels disappearing into the belly of the building.

I go to the drawer, take the bundle of notes, toss it into a bag with a couple of shirts, trousers, underwear. That's all I need to start again.

I feel better. I'm not going to do it, I don't want to die. I'm not going to go crazy either. I'll wait until night and go out, catch a bus to Rocha, on the border with Brazil. I'll cross by foot, go to the bus station, decide which city to make for. I'll sleep along the way. Perhaps somewhere else I can stop being a coward.

I no longer feel the ball tied to my neck. I no longer want to die.

XIX

Another bright day in the middle of winter. Ursula leaves her apartment, places the blue suitcase outside, makes sure the door is properly closed, and turns the key in all three of the locks. Few people can imagine what a difficult place the world is for a middle-aged woman who lives alone, but she knows all too well. She can't relax her guard for an instant, can't wander down the street lost in thought; a few years ago, a couple of thugs pushed her to the ground and stole her bag. Although the woman coming down the stairs today is not the same one who was the victim of a mugging only two years ago; now she keeps her wits about her as she walks down the street, and in her bag, between the bottle of water and her woollen cardigan, is a .38.

She descends the marble stairs, we were saying, very carefully; in front of her is the suitcase, which must be heavy because it bumps loudly on each step. Logically, the descent will take longer than usual.

By the time she reaches the hall she is perspiring, and she casts a sad glance at the elevator, stuck between floors; it's been months, almost a year now, that it's been there, paralysed because the service company can't get hold of the parts. They've already told the owners they'll have to replace the motor with something more modern, because this is an old one that isn't manufactured any more, and it will take three months for the new one to arrive. And they've said it will be very expensive, of course.

In this godforsaken world, honest owners who can't afford the rising costs are pushed out and so the process of gentrification begins. She read that somewhere, she can't remember where. Out of the corner of her eye she measures the mountain of garbage that every day grows larger, at the bottom of the shaft. Her neighbours are a filthy lot, chucking paper and chewing gum down there; she wouldn't be surprised if there are condoms, too.

She wheels the suitcase out into the street, into the unseasonal temperatures of this Indian summer, and is warmed by the rays of the sun.

Opposite, at a bar with tables on the sidewalk, the woman in the blue coat who is drinking coffee observes Ursula walk past, takes out some money and leaves it next to her cup. She waits until Ursula has passed, picks up her bag and her phone, stands up and follows her at a safe distance. Ursula stops at the corner, adjusts the position of the suitcase, puts on her sunglasses, glances casually left and right, spots the woman.

She checks the inside pocket of her jacket: the car key is there.

The woman in the blue coat stops too, checks the time, does up her buttons, takes out her phone and makes a call that lasts less than fifteen seconds.

At the corner of Sarandí and Treinta y Tres, Ursula turns left, walks a couple of hundred yards to the entrance to the parking garage where she now keeps her car, walks past Alicia, who is sitting behind the payment window, and greets her with a comment about the good weather and how long it's going to last.

She thought it would be easier to lift the suitcase and put it in the back of the car; she has two or three attempts, but without success. She looks to both sides. She also thought there would always be someone to take pity on a middle-aged woman struggling with a bulky case. And she wasn't wrong; a young man who has just got out of a red Toyota runs over to help.

"Can I give you a hand?"

"That's very kind of you."

"Don't worry, I've got it."

Uruguayans, she thinks, always so chivalrous. It never fails: they can't see a woman in distress without fanning out their feathers like peacocks.

"This weighs a ton! Have you got a case full of bricks?"

"Paper is heavier than you'd think."

"You must have a whole library in here." The lad looks at her and she smiles back. Ursula thanks him for his help and wishes him a good day, gets into her car and starts the engine.

Now she is driving along the waterfront out of the city centre and heading east; she drives and she thinks there was another path she could have taken, the possibility of being a different person, but she doesn't regret being here and doing what she is about to do. She also thinks it is never too late to imagine a different life.

The beach season and the tourists are long gone; today there is just the grime and pollution the tide has washed up on the shoreline.

Ursula looks in her rear-view mirror, adjusts it when she

stops at the lights: she has seen that black Fiat before. It's not very close, perhaps fifty yards away.

She turns left, then takes Avenida General Rivera; in a few minutes she'll arrive at her destination. The avenue, named after the man who exterminated the indigenous population of what today is the territory of Uruguay, runs parallel to the seafront and crosses the city from one side to the other.

Finding a spot a hundred yards from the port, she parks the car, locks it. She observes the cars approaching from the west, sees the black Fiat, which stops a little further on, sees the woman in the blue coat.

She takes the suitcase out of the car, with far less of a struggle than when she put it in. Finally, she crosses the road, passes through the main entrance with its three arches, walks down the central pathway, and then takes a side path and disappears among the cypresses and monuments of Buceo Cemetery.

XX

Antinucci crosses Plaza Independencia in the direction of the Old Town, heading for his office. Leaving behind the statue of General Artigas, he looks both ways before passing through the Puerta de la Ciudadela. His overcoat is open, there are a few drops of sweat on his forehead, he looks as if he is tired of life.

He misses his routine from the times before the day of that accursed robbery, the way one misses a childhood summer home, a friend who has died in an accident, or a lover who entered a convent.

Ursula wasn't wrong when she uttered those terrible words, when she spat at him that all his strategies had been wrong, *inefficient*, she said, and the lawyer clenches his fists when he remembers the precise expression the woman used to talk about his organization of the operation, of the robbery. A right hook to the jaw that he can still feel, the word still lodged inside his head.

He tries to forget, to concentrate on his surroundings, he looks at the reflection of the sun on the cobbles of Calle Sarandí, tries to focus his attention on the beauty of the art nouveau forms of the Edificio Pablo Ferrando, which today houses a bookstore. He approaches the beautiful curved windows, runs his eyes over the building, enters with no particular purpose, just to kill time, distractedly leafs through a couple of crime novels. He decides to buy one called *Crocodile Tears*, perhaps because he likes the title or the cover. He pays and leaves, walks towards Plaza Matriz, enters the building, goes up three floors in the elevator, unlocks the door.

This time he's going to make sure the whole operation goes to plan, that it doesn't all go awry like the assault on the armoured truck. He thinks about the robbery and Ursula's face appears, Ursula's words. Damn her.

He's prepared to do whatever it takes; if he has to use violence, he'll use violence; if he has to shoot, he'll shoot. And if he has to kill people then he'll kill, because there's a lot of money at stake and it's worth every drop of blood that has to be spilled. He's not going to be a coward like Inspector Clemen.

He enters his office. He's alone.

Be careful: a shopping mall is full of innocent people, Clemen said. The world is full of hypocrites. He laughs at these politically correct ideas and suspects that the vast majority of humanity would not hesitate to fire at innocent bystanders if there were anything to be gained from it. He is familiar with Clemen and his ilk, with their virtue signalling. All so very proper, shocked by death, by violence, but deep down they don't give a damn. Anyway, he knows nobody is truly innocent.

Antinucci is not ashamed to say he believes in violence, in guns. Haven't all this democracy and pacifism demonstrated their own futility? Dogs will tear each other apart if you don't rule them with a big stick. God and the bosses, he argues, in that order.

He opens all the windows; the place was fumigated yesterday and there is a smell of insecticide. And also the lingering odour of tobacco trapped between these walls. Added to which, it's a warm day, weather that seems set to continue for a few more hours.

Antinucci wipes his forehead, takes an antacid tablet and a mint from his pocket and pops them into his mouth, one after the other. He swallows the tablet and sucks the mint. He feels a pressing need to smoke, a need that extends throughout his body and makes him wonder if he will manage to stick to his decision.

His phone rings and he takes it out of his pocket. He is coming to hate these devices.

"Yes, Clemen, I called you earlier. Two things. First: check the woman's apartment, turn it upside down if necessary, they need to make sure the money isn't there. I don't know, send a locksmith. You don't have a warrant? Well, send a burglar then, I don't know! Second: the operation is scheduled for Wednesday at three o'clock. I need some uniformed officers at each door, each access point to Punta Carretas. And some plain-clothes agents inside. At all levels. Yes, I think we'll need about thirty officers. Properly equipped, armed to the teeth. And some patrol cars, at least ten. What do you mean, you can't allocate so many agents and so many cars? Clemen, let's get this straight: everything is at stake here. Yes, she's bringing the money, and I'm going to hand over her sister. No, we have to be prepared for any eventuality, I can't make do with a group of cops from some neighbourhood police station. I need people who are intelligent, highly trained, in good physical condition. I need agents to monitor them inside the building and to block all the exits. Think about it – what if she escapes? Because this woman is highly dangerous and we don't know what she might come up with. Imagine if she gets away with the money again. I wouldn't be surprised, knowing her. We have to be prepared. What do you mean, you don't have that many people and not with that kind of training? Inspector, it's not as if I'm asking you for an army, I just want to do things properly for once. Is that too much to ask? And if the minister kicks up a fuss, make something up. Tell him you've tracked down one of those Italian narcos who escaped from prison and is on the run, that you have to surround and arrest him because he's dangerous. Or that you've been given a tip-off about the guy who murdered the Candyman, for example. Well, if he's not important enough to justify mobilizing so many people, we'll think of someone else. What about that banker who swindled the jet set, ran off to the Cayman Islands? We could say he's been spotted in Montevideo. What do you think? Is that too much? I don't know, it's up to you, you're the expert, I'm just asking you to send me the best people you've got. Not Captain Lima, definitely not."

Antinucci ends the call and throws the phone angrily down on his desk. He looks at his watch. He remembers that his secretary will be back in half an hour, and he can scarcely contain his erection. He wards off the temptations of the flesh. He would like to pray properly and commend himself to God but makes do with mumbling a quick prayer.

All Glory to God. Amen.

Wednesday will be a big day.

THE DAY
OF THE ESCAPE

14.50

Ursula drags the suitcase up the ramp and passes through the main entrance to Punta Carretas Shopping, the one from Calle Ellauri. She goes through the section where the clothing and jewellery stores are, past a group of North American tourists, a gaggle of noisy preschoolers accompanied by their teachers, and three guards employed by a firm called Royal Security.

The tallest of the guards flashes her a brief smile and Ursula smiles back. Not even the security cameras will record these gestures.

Ursula walks quickly, she is comfortably dressed, she is wearing running shoes, she has a pink leather bag over her shoulder, and to judge by her appearance she seems to know exactly where she is going.

She still feels a little queasy from last night's overindulgence, her raid on the fridge, but nothing will stop her from implementing her plans.

Stopping for some ten minutes next to the central stairway, she looks at her watch several times, waits until the agreed time. The nerves are starting to get to her. She waits with the same anxiety with which she awaited Daddy's footsteps on those mornings after the night of penitence, when she waited, confined and in the darkness, for the sound that indicated he was about to open the door. She waits as she did before, her rage under tight control in her breast, just as she waited for Diego's phone call for thirty long days, tortured by the shadow of doubt. She waits with the same anxiety with which she awaited the arrival of Antinucci, her muscles tense and her guard up, in a state of war, on permanent alert. Because Ursula knows how to wait. Because Ursula has spent her whole lifetime waiting.

And she also knows that this waiting is the worst part, these endless minutes, her nerves on edge and her brain brimming with images of disaster.

15.00

She checks the time again and finally nods, continues until she reaches the escalator a little further from the entrance, almost in the centre of the mall. She feels a brief stabbing pain in her left knee, her lips tighten in a grimace of disgust or annoyance, a furrow appears on her brow, she makes a note to herself not to put off her visit to the doctor; she is no longer twenty years old, and tomorrow or the day after she'll call to make an appointment. She thinks about this task and impatiently switches the pink bag from her right shoulder to her left. She walks past the jeweller's she likes so much, glances at the window display, the wristwatch she covets, smiles to herself as she notes that it is still in its place, waiting for her. I'll be back for you, my darling, she thinks.

Before she reaches the escalator, she leans over the railing and towards the floor below, scanning the huge space until she locates Luz and Antinucci, close together, looking up. When she makes out her sister, something loosens inside her and she sighs in relief.

The lawyer registers her presence and juts his chin forward. Ursula understands that he is signalling in Luz's direction, and interprets the message: *See? I've got your sister. Now we can do the handover.*

Antinucci juts his chin again, this time in the direction of the gunman off to his left, who responds with a small movement of his index finger, a gesture of recognition or warning.

She calculates the distances. Luz and her captor are some twenty yards from the foot of the escalator she has just begun to descend. She observes the man watching from the left, her gaze coming to rest on the sports bag sitting on the handrail, and the man turns the bag so it is pointing towards her. Down below, the lawyer walks right next to Luz; they have the air of a married couple or a pair of lovers indulging in a spot of window-shopping, and now they look up and see her coming down, look at her with that air of forced happiness, casual and relaxed, that families adopt when they are in malls.

They see her and give no sign of recognition.

Ursula follows the instructions she agreed with the lawyer in the park. She catches the elevator down to Level 0, keeping a firm grasp on the suitcase in front of her, one step below.

How strange; now the action has started she doesn't feel anything, as if none of this was actually happening to her. Perhaps in a few years' time she will record these events, this scene with more excitement, more disquiet than she feels now. In the middle of her descent, however, Ursula thinks that this is her story, that for the first time this is her own story, that right now she is the protagonist of an adventure that belongs to her, of a quest she invented or unleashed or at least contributed to. And finally she realizes, not without a sense of regret, that for her own safety and that of her sister, the chronicle of these events can only ever be recounted as an anonymous tale centring around an unnamed woman.

She tries to convince herself it doesn't matter, that fame is a myth, that afterwards all we have is the memory of past pleasures; she repeats tango lyrics that, as we know, never tell the truth. She sighs, resigned to pass namelessly into history, she sighs and grips the handle of the case tight, clutching the pink bag to her body; she looks again at her sister, whose eyes are wide open as she observes, unblinking, this eternal descent down this almost infinite escalator.

When she reaches Level 0, a large group of German or Swedish or Dutch tourists appears; the tourists are listening attentively to the guide's explanations about the old prison on the site of which this mall was built, looking around with a mixture of curiosity and admiration, asking questions and walking slowly behind the woman who is talking, pointing and answering.

Ursula moves through the crowd of people, apologizes in three languages, thinks she catches the words 'dungeon' and 'prison', is sure she hears the name of José "Pepe" Mujica, the country's former president who was also once an inmate here. Then, very slowly and as if by chance, she approaches the couple who appear to be window-shopping.

She has one eye on the movements of Antinucci, who is keeping Luz close by his side; the other eye is on the gunman on Level 1, behind the sports bag he swivels as she advances.

The couple are not far from the service area, no more than fifteen or twenty yards, a distance she calculates she can traverse in less time than she originally calculated. This despite the fact that the suitcase is a hindrance, as are her extra pounds and her lack of physical fitness. Later today, within just a few minutes, these details will acquire another dimension in this story.

Ursula pushes aside such thoughts of excess flesh and neglected exercise routines; she lowers her gaze, focusing on the suitcase and on the need to keep moving.

When she looks up, she knows it is time to begin.

15.01

The following events occur: Ursula takes twenty-seven paces over to where Luz and Antinucci are, the large suitcase shielding her body. Now, as agreed, she will wait until the gunman moves from his position on Level 1 down to Level 0. There is nothing they need to say, nothing not already agreed in their meeting in the park.

For the thousandth time, she goes over Antinucci's instructions.

The first step is to go to the service area, a closed room used as a baby-changing facility and which is at the end of a corridor. Antinucci, Ursula and Luz will go in, with the suitcase.

The second step is to open the case and check all the money is there.

The third step is to release Luz, who will leave with Ursula.

This third step depends on the success of the preceding one, Antinucci's approval, and will take place under the supervision of the gunman, posted at the end of the corridor and with his rifle trained on the door of the changing room, which has no other exit. The two women will have no choice but to walk past him. A deadly trap, should they try to escape.

As we were saying, Ursula is standing near Luz and the lawyer, clutching the suitcase with both hands. And that's when she hears it, when she hears his voice. *Be careful, Ursula, be very careful what you do. What need was there to get involved with these criminals? What need was there to put your sister's life in danger?* Be quiet, Daddy, be quiet. This has nothing to do with you, be quiet and go away, I can't listen to you now, get back to your grave because I have no intention of listening to you. *And all for money. What good will the money do you, if something happens to Luz? So much risk, so much danger just to have a big house and expensive slimming treatments.* Be quiet, Daddy, I told you to be quiet.

She won't listen to him any more, won't hear his words, the old bastard. She looks without seeing, trembles with rage, her teeth chattering. Leave me in peace, get back to your grave and don't bother me again, Daddy. She grips the handles tighter, clenches her jaw. Luz and Antinucci are right in front of her, she could reach out and touch them.

And now Ursula rushes and makes a mistake.

She puts her right hand in her pocket, takes something out and just then, just as she is extracting a black shiny object from its hiding place, she detects something unexpected, realizes something is wrong: a short chain, metal links joining Luz to Antinucci and with a handcuff at either end, soldering the man's left hand to her sister's right.

When she understands the situation, when her mind processes the unexpected detail of the handcuffs, it will already be too late; she will have taken out the black shiny object, will be holding it in her hand, and her hand will be raised so it is level with the lawyer's forehead. He will observe the silvery black shiny object before his eyes, and Ursula will suspect she has unleashed something unstoppable, she will know there is no turning back when she registers the expression of alarm on the lawyer's face, the immobile surprise in his gaze as he stares at the hand and the object, which is also immobile at the height of the man's head.

The clamour of the shoppers and the background music fall silent inside her head, everything disappears except for the scene which she is at the centre of, and she has the fleeting sensation of staring into the abyss.

Time blurs, it dissolves. She releases the handle of the case. She knows it is too late to abandon her plan. So she shouts at the top of her voice.

"Close your eyes, Luz, as tight as you can."

15.03

The hand that holds the pepper spray brings it closer to the lawyer's face, the finger squeezes tight, spraying the contents of the can into Antinucci's eyes and mouth.

"You goddamn fucking bitch..." The lawyer shouts, swears, groans, his words gradually giving way to howls of pain.

The index finger continues to press the button, squeezing with all its strength, emptying the contents of the container into the face of the man who is screaming and trying to protect himself, backing away. He tries to shield himself with his hands but it's too late, he's defenceless. Ursula grabs his lapels, holds him, immobilizes him and continues to spray; mercilessly, she discharges the substance into his face until there is nothing left, until there is just the hissing of the empty canister. Antinucci's eyes are closed and he is hunched over, crying and coughing as a result of the capsaicin, a compound derived from the fruits of plants belonging to the genus capsicum, the active component of chilli peppers, which causes an immediate burning sensation in the eyes, irritation of the mucous membranes, respiratory difficulties and itching.

Luz, who got as far away from the lawyer as possible, who squeezed her eyelids shut like her sister told her and tried to cover her face with her free hand, with her arm, with the fabric of her coat and who thus avoided being sprayed, now observes the scene in alarm, still trying to keep her distance from Antinucci.

Ursula sees that the lawyer is suffering the immediate effects of the pepper spray, knows he will soon experience inflammation of the membranes of the eyes, the nose, the mouth and the lungs, that the burning sensation will be intense, instant and overwhelming, that it will cause or has already caused temporary blindness.

She watches as he twists and turns, shouts and coughs and groans, she sees the tears welling up through his tightly closed eyelids.

The man's cry starts as a low groan, rising in volume and tone as the pain intensifies, expanding through the immense space of the shopping mall, rises higher and higher, reaches the escalator and the ears of the gunman.

When Antinucci emitted his first cry, the gunman, who had already begun his descent, neither saw nor heard him. He has his own problems: he is in the middle of a crush of people who are shouting and moving, dancing and pushing, because today the crowd in the mall includes a Brazilian samba troupe who are travelling en masse, in glorious Technicolor. It seems that this mall attracts people who are not particularly concerned by the issue of sound pollution, people who are happy to communicate with each other at the tops of their voices.

The gunman looks in irritation at the tourists crowding around him, tries to fend them off with his elbows and his arms, perhaps he says something, curses them or demands a little respect, and at first he doesn't hear Antinucci's cries or maybe he confuses them with the samba, *pagode, axé* or whatever the enthusiastic foreigners are singing.

Then he turns his attention back to the lawyer and sees the transformation, his face a mask of pain; he watches the man frantically rub his eyes. He also sees the woman with the canister in her hand, and his brain establishes a connection of cause and effect. A second later, Antinucci's cries reach the gunman's ears, but he has already seen everything he needed to see and goes into action with his hand on the zip of the sports bag.

Let us return to Ursula, who is holding the empty canister and observes the lawyer's movements. Why on earth didn't she realize Antinucci might handcuff Luz to himself?

She thinks that everything has gone wrong.

Ursula angrily hurls the container to the ground, watches it roll away. And she sees the man with the black bag on the escalator, his hand on the zip.

227

The gunman, his grey hair combed back, dressed in a pinstripe suit like someone in a gangster movie, having spotted Antinucci's contortions and seeing Ursula with the spray in her hand, understands that things are not going to plan. He unzips the bag, takes out a weapon, and from where he stands halfway down the escalator trains it on his target, on Ursula.

She sees what he is doing and understands she has to make sure she doesn't present an easy target, she has to move: better still, she has to take shelter. She lets go of the suitcase and runs with an agility one would not have imagined her to possess. The shot intended for her hits the ground, the bullet bounces off the hard tiles, describes an arc through the air and passes inches from the head of a child who is holding his mother's hand and will never know how lucky he was to have bent down to pick up a teddy bear that had fallen to the floor. The sound, it goes without saying, is lost in the hubbub.

In four strides, Ursula has disappeared among the tourists. The visitors, oblivious to events on the escalator, unaware of what so far is the only shot to have been fired, continue to listen attentively to the guide's explanations.

Ursula stops and checks the gunman, sees that he is standing halfway down the now immobile escalator, that he is tracking her with the barrel of his gun, taking aim for a second time. He stops.

Things aren't going to plan.

The first shot has not activated any alarms and nor has it been seen or heard by the security guards, but it has been spotted by two members of the Brazilian samba troupe, who are just behind the armed man. The Brazilians scream with terror and struggle to retreat, going against the flow of the crowds and of the escalator itself.

"Help! Help!"

They try to put some distance between themselves and the conflict, calling for assistance, desperate to force their way back up the stairway. They try, we say, but in vain because nobody moves: the crowd, unaware of what is going on, don't even stop talking. The Brazilians – a gay couple with impressive physiques, their muscles rippling beneath their tracksuits – try to push their way through. Today, the atriums, walkways, stores, bars and of course the stairs are jam-packed with people: and the Brazilians are unable to move so much as an inch. They exchange a few words, calculate the odds and, like the athletes they appear to be, jump over the handrail and down, a drop of several feet – landing in the middle of a bar that serves fresh fruit juice and gluten-free bread – and run for the nearest exit.

Meanwhile, a second shot is fired and this time – due to some strange acoustic miracle – it is heard by the crowd on the escalator and even by the German tourists who, a little further off, stop paying attention to the guide and search instead for the origin of the disturbance and for the security guards. Ursula hears it too, from where she has taken refuge behind a pillar. This second shot unleashes chaos: on the escalator, some want to go up and some want to go down. There is pushing and shoving, but nobody can move.

Downstairs, on Level 0, people who a few seconds ago were walking about, looking in store windows or drinking *mate*, are now shouting and rushing around, running this way and that, grabbing their children and attempting to flee from what they think is a shoot-out.

15.06

Let us go back to Antinucci: his face is contorted, he is hunched over, rubbing his eyes wildly, scarcely able to move, tied to Luz by the shortest of chains.

The burning sensation is unbearable, his eyes and nose and mouth are on fire; and although he is coughing and the pain is all-consuming, he hears the sound of the shot and his desperation grows. Where's that gunman? Why isn't he here? Is he yet another moron, like all the rest of them? Is there nobody in this country who can do a job properly? And where are the police Clemen was going to send? Just for good measure, his eyelids, which are already on the fleshy side, have turned into two red balls that give him a monstrous appearance, like something from a teen horror movie.

Ursula, some twenty-five or thirty yards away, sheltering behind her column, observes and shakes her head. What kind of a world are we living in? You go out and there's no guarantee you'll come back home alive, every man and his dog has a gun, there's no shortage of maniacs happy to open fire in broad daylight. What a godforsaken world we live in. The operation to rescue Luz has gone wrong, she thinks, she has to calm down, to put her thoughts in order. The first thing to do is separate Luz from Antinucci, but how?

You got her into this, Ursula. You have to get her out of it. But Daddy, I never imagined I'd have to deal with this, never expected the lawyer to handcuff her to himself, nobody could have predicted that. *Do something, Ursula. Luz's life is in danger and it's your fault.* Be quiet, Daddy! I'm trying to think of a solution.

Ursula thinks as fast as she can, imagining objects like tongs and shears and pliers, but obviously she has nothing like that in her pink bag, just a bottle of water, a powerful flashlight, a cardigan in case it gets cold, a plastic package with ten thousand dollars, and the .38 she retrieved from behind the loose tile last night. Nothing that could help her cut a chain.

She realizes she is afraid, but the fear she feels is not the normal kind: it's strange, almost enjoyable, akin to a feeling of vertigo, tinged with ecstasy, a feeling very close to pleasure. The air that runs across her back turns damp, warm. She sighs.

Meanwhile, Luz, joined to Antinucci by a metal umbilical cord, hasn't wasted her time: she has taken advantage of the lawyer's blindness, his desperation, his confusion; and while he writhes in agony and rubs his face with his right hand, she swallows her panic, extends her fingers and reaches into the man's left pocket, the one next to the chain that binds them together. She touches a wallet, two phones and something that feels like a bunch of keys. They are indeed keys but, after a fleeting moment of excitement, her fingers touch them, examine them, and the keys turn out to be too large; perhaps they are for a car or for the lawyer's house.

Luz takes out the telephones – one is hers and she puts it in her pocket, returning the other to its place. Her hand explores a little further: coins, pieces of paper, nothing. To search the other pocket, the one on the right, she has to pass either in front of or behind the man and use her left hand.

She decides to pass behind Antinucci's back, it seems more discreet, although from the way he is writhing and screaming and coughing it is obvious her captor is in no condition to attend to the movements of his captive. The restrictions on her movements mean she has to turn around so she and the lawyer are back-to-back, and in this position she turns her head somewhat uncomfortably.

Luz overcomes her fear and discomfort, and even appears to find a reserve of cold calculation somewhere inside herself, the effect of the adrenaline, no doubt. She is alert, constantly surveying her surroundings even though nobody seems to have noticed her manoeuvres yet. The sniper is concentrating on Ursula, on following her movements, but for now she appears to be safe behind that pillar. Luz inserts her hand into the pocket of the man who cannot open his eyes; she feels the cloth, delves around. The pocket is empty, save for one small object: a key. She swiftly extracts it, looks at it and then at the handcuffs: she's sure this is the key.

She has it.

15.07

Just then, the police enter the mall, a patrol of ten officers, five men and five women because we also need to ensure we meet the gender quota in our story. The squadron bursts into the mall through the main entrance on Level 1, which opens onto Calle Ellauri; and after seeing the crowds going down the escalators, head for the main stairway. It won't be long before they, too, reach Level 0 and join the action.

15.08

Luz's hand is shaking, either from the effort or from nerves; her fingers tremble, and there is nothing she can do to still them. To make matters worse, inserting a small key into an equally small lock is no easy task if you are over forty and suffer from a degree of long-sightedness, an inability to focus on objects that are close up, an optician's prescription of 2 or 2.5. And without the aid of her glasses. Luz doesn't manage to find the hole and becomes increasingly nervous. She takes a deep breath and tries again. She calms down.

Antinucci still has his eyes closed, is still in pain, but he stopped shouting when the second shot went off and now he is listening; he suspects, is sure even, that things are going badly, that his plan has gone to hell. He senses that Luz is moving around him and doesn't understand why; he gropes around for the woman, swiping at the air. Luz feels a hand slapping her shoulder, is startled and drops the key, which falls to the ground, bounces on the tiles and comes to rest some three or four yards away.

Let us pause and capture the scene, take a photograph of the space and our characters at this precise point in time. Our pair of Brazilians ran for the exit and disappeared from the scene, and we will hear no more about them in this story. After the second shot went off, the rest of the samba troupe reached Level 0 and scattered. The gunman, who lost sight of the woman with the spray, is walking towards Luz and Antinucci, his head high, alert to any movement. Ursula is sheltering behind a pillar and contemplating her next step. The forces of law and order have spread out and are preparing to go down the main stairway. Luz is staring at the keys three or four yards away, so near yet so far, and she wonders how she can get closer to them without alerting the lawyer's suspicions. Antinucci is motionless, his eyes closed, his back hunched, alert to the sounds around him but reassured when he confirms that Luz is still there.

There are groups of people running hither and thither. It's a confusing scene, and Ursula takes advantage of the confusion to come out from behind the pillar. She searches for something with her gaze, she finds it.

Without taking her eyes from the gunman, she walks towards an employee in a Royal Security uniform, the guard who we earlier saw exchange a smile with Ursula. It doesn't appear to be chance that he is there, so close to everything that is happening. They swap a few words. He nods, they separate and he heads for the service area.

Ursula looks over towards Luz, towards the gunman approaching her sister. She bites her lip. She rummages in her pink bag, walks towards them.

15.09

Luz sees the man with the gun and takes a decision. She pulls, getting as far as she can from Antinucci. Though the metal of the handcuff cuts into her wrist she doesn't give in to the pain, instead she pulls harder, dragging the lawyer a couple of yards; her arm is at full stretch yet she is still a few inches short, a final fraction. She extends her fingers as far as she can but it's no good.

Antinucci, alert despite his suffering, pulls in the opposite direction. He shouts: "What's going on? Why are you pulling? Even if you manage to get away from me, you won't get out of here alive. I already told your sister: you won't get out of here alive. Did you hear me? There's no way out."

Luz's desperation grows as the man with the gun approaches. She swallows, takes something from her own pocket, pulls again, gets as far as she can from Antinucci. She tenses her muscles in one final effort, extends her fingers with the object she holds in her hand – a granola bar – uses it to bridge the gap and pull the key towards her, grabs it and this time slots it neatly into the hole. She hears the click of the handcuffs opening.

"What's happening? That fucking bitch. Is she getting away? The goddamn bitch is getting away!" Luz is running from Antinucci when she sees the gunman, no more than ten yards away, approaching and pointing his gun at her. She stares at the barrel of the rifle.

"Stop or I'll shoot."

Antinucci hears the man, hears the threat. In the midst of the storm, he touches his wrist and confirms that Luz has escaped. He is still blind, his eyes still burning.

"You finally showed up, Cacho. I thought you'd gone off on holiday."

"I'm here."

"Grab her. Apparently she wants to leave before we've finished."

The gunman (but let us call him Cacho, now we know that's what he's called) takes the woman roughly by the arm and, still pointing his weapon at her, turns to Antinucci, perhaps to ask for instructions.

Just then all three of them hear a voice. They all look up at once.

"Let her go. I'm not going to tell you twice."

The voice is unyielding, as hard as the revolver Cacho feels pressing into his back.

Antinucci, who is blind but not deaf, shouts back, "Don't do anything stupid, Ursula. This place is surrounded by the police. There are agents everywhere, there's no escape."

15.11

The tune playing on the loudspeakers until a few seconds ago has now stopped, replaced by crackles and whistles, background murmurings, the sound of coughing and of throats being cleared.

Finally, a voice says "Hello, hello, hello", in a tone reminiscent of the soundcheck at a concert, and perhaps some of those listening who have not yet noticed anything amiss might think a performance is about to start. But no, in a few seconds everyone will realize something unusual is happening, something a very long way from the ideal of safety and happiness represented by a shopping trip.

Over the loudspeakers comes a voice that seems unprepared for the occasion, with little modulation, stumbling over the words with the diction of one unaccustomed to having a microphone placed in front of them. As if reading out instructions.

"All shoppers who are on Level 0, please make your way to the nearest exit in an orderly fashion. Thank you."

And this is all those in charge of the mall do in response to the uproar. Because the mall is just a reflection of what happens in our society, and indifference or evasion in response to the sufferings of its customers appears to be included in the establishment's operating manual.

But let us ignore the loudspeakers and go back a few seconds, to the moment Antinucci realized Luz had got away. The lawyer is doubled up with pain, shouting threats. Luz is still, her eyes on the gunman who is gripping her arm and pointing his weapon at her. Tears of impotence run down her cheeks. Everyone hears the hard, unyielding voice, and they all raise their heads at once.

"Let her go. I'm not going to tell you twice." Ursula's revolver digs into the gunman's back.

He releases Luz. Antinucci shouts: "Don't be foolish, Ursula. This place is surrounded by police. There are agents everywhere, there's no escape. Stop them, Cacho."

Ursula raises her gun and points it at Cacho, level with his head: everyone hears the familiar sound of a revolver being cocked.

Cacho hears it too, and instantly throws himself to the ground, covering his skull with his hands. Because, yes, the survival instinct can expose even the toughest of characters, even those who have been hardened by a calling such as his.

Ursula turns to her sister. "Come on, Luz, run. Follow me." The sisters disappear into the crowd as the police arrive at Level 0.

The agents talk to each other, point, nod and fan out. Some run right, others run left.

The gunman, on the floor, still holding his weapon, hears the sound of boots approaching and a voice, a shout of warning.

"You're surrounded. Let go of your weapon."

15.15

Before continuing, we should make a small digression. The quality of construction of the different zones of this and every other mall in the world is directly proportionate to the flow of people: the public areas are constructed using materials such as marble and wood, high-quality floors, excellent finishes.

The service sectors, which see less traffic, such as bathrooms and corridors, areas where there are no stores, are more modest; and if we could enter those parts off limits to the public, we would see they are, frankly, neglected. Although nobody is concerned about the state of those places because nobody sees them: they are separated from the sectors open to the public, hidden away at the end of labyrinthine corridors, almost inaccessible to shoppers.

To reach this restricted zone, Ursula and Luz have to go through the service area, leave the bathrooms behind them, walk down a poorly lit corridor and find an almost invisible door only accessible, as the notice says, to authorized personnel. Here, Nicolás is waiting for them. They exchange silent signals; the lad looks around and closes the door behind them.

The three hurry through another maze of corridors with peeling paint and loose tiles, a world that does not seem to be part of the same building. They turn right and then left, enter a small windowless room; the guard brings up the rear and closes the door behind him, then points to a metal filing cabinet. "You need to help me shift that, without making too much noise. Afterwards, I'll see if I can slide it back into place on my own."

Between the three of them they silently move it.

15.17

Behind the filing cabinet and a little above floor height is a small opening, covered by a hatch, which could lead to the heating vents or the air conditioning or the sewers. Nicolás pulls the handle and the hatch swings open; all the women can see is a dark hole. The lad looks at Ursula, who looks at Luz.

The tunnel is open, waiting for them.

Ursula pushes Luz through, then follows her. The hole swallows them.

Five minutes later, Nicolás will enter the staff changing room, wash his hands, open his locker, change out of his uniform; his shift is finally over.

In a few minutes he will come out into the central atrium and see the chaos, the disorder, the people filming on their phones, watching the police patrol take two men away: one of them with his eyes closed, the other in a pinstripe suit, both shouting that there's been a mistake, giving explanations the authorities appear to ignore, as they are bundled into separate patrol cars.

The presence of a large suitcase, presumably linked to the criminal activity of the two suspects, requires the mall to be emptied for at least an hour.

That's the protocol: when an abandoned object is detected in a public space, particularly if it is a bag or a case or a box, it is automatically classified as dangerous.

The special forces arrive at a jog and, dressed in black, inspect the object and decide what to do; they clear the area, cordon it off, stop the traffic in the vicinity. After a range of scientific tests, the case is found to contain books tied together with tape, all packed tightly together. The case is sent to the lost property office, in the hope somebody will claim it.

By the time this happens, Nicolás will already have left by a side door, crossed Calle Solano García and entered a small and somewhat neglected garden on the other side of the road. We will lose sight of him for a while.

THE ESCAPE

Ursula doesn't hesitate or give way to the temptation to look back: she pushes Luz, the two of them go in, and the jaws of the tunnel clamp shut. They leave behind them the brightly lit stores, the colourful clothes, the television sets, a world full of people, the background music and the voices of the crowd. They don't leave behind the fear, though. It clings to their clothes, permeates their sweat, constricts their throats.

The two women disappear into the most absolute darkness, the scene fades to black, the sound recedes, something hard to imagine in our world so full of stimuli.

Ursula turns on the flashlight, holds it up, tries to push back the darkness, make it less terrifying. Luz goes ahead, trying to light her way with the glow from her phone screen. They crawl forward, knees, elbows and palms on the floor, concentrating on the effort.

They feel their way along the walls; the floor and ceiling are uneven and stony. Some parts are damp as if water was leaking in, while others are dry.

The space is narrow, an almost circular shaft. For the first few yards they feel as if they are suffocating, although this tunnel ventilates through the other tunnel, the one the anarchists dug, and there is also a pipe that connects to the exterior. Here, we should pause to explain that on 18 March 1931 a group of anarchists escaped from Punta Carretas Prison through a tunnel built from outside the jail, from a coal merchant's by the name of El Buen Trato.

Imagine what it is like to crawl through a gallery scarcely larger than your body, a narrow dark corridor with no end in sight. Think about the sense of suffocation that comes from being buried alive deep in the belly of the earth, entombed in a long tunnel, with several yards of soil and asphalt and buildings above your head.

They aren't cowards or shrinking violets, but how can they go forward if they know that the slightest slip, the merest movement could make this place into their tomb?

They crawl along in silence, advancing with difficulty. At first, they crawl downhill, their senses adapt to the confinement, and the suffocating sensation begins to fade.

They don't talk; each of them is locked in her own thoughts, her own concerns.

Ursula feels the terror of what they have been through start to fade, and she concentrates on the money from the hold-up, thinks about all that money. *It's my money, Daddy, be quiet.*

Luz, although she prefers not to think about what has happened, can't help being afraid and, even if she doesn't show it, is thinking about how close she has just come to dying.

With differences and in silence, mingled with other thoughts, both of them are going through their respective memories of this tunnel, the history they heard and read about at home, at school and in the media: Operation El

Abuso. They – and every other Uruguayan – know that almost fifty years ago, one hundred and eleven Tupamaros tunnelled their way out of Punta Carretas Prison, the jail that once stood on the site now occupied by the shopping mall from which they have just escaped.

They both remember, almost simultaneously, recalling the same images from the television and the newspapers. However, memory is a strange and mysterious thing, and what for one is almost a cowboy movie is, for the other, a heroic chapter in the history of our country.

Ursula and Luz are forty-eight and forty-five years old, respectively, and this fact would not be important were it not for the effort, the physical demands imposed by crawling down a rough, narrow passageway, which initially descends, then is level, and ends with an uphill section.

Luz manages it from the start. She has been going to the gym for years, she is in good condition. Her sister, though, is being pushed forward by the adrenaline produced by a mixture of fear and anger, and she is on the verge of exhaustion.

They are silent because they need to conserve all their strength to keep moving forward, to keep gaining ground, to save themselves from going mad in this black hole. They know it's only fifty yards to the exit.

If they make it to the exit.

If the earth doesn't devour them first.

When they entered, when they got inside this tunnel, when they were swallowed up by the dark, Ursula shuddered with fear as she remembered Daddy's punishments. The feeling took her by surprise.

She is disturbed by the way her old memories insist on surfacing at a time such as this, as if the past had not died, as if he had not died. She tries to draw a veil over it, but the dark, dense fog creeps around the edges.

You deserved it, Ursula. You were a disobedient child. And you were twisted and manipulative, Daddy. *How would you have turned out without those punishments, my darling Ursula? You wouldn't just be fat, you'd be a whale.* Go away, Daddy. Go back to your grave and don't bother the living, go back to that place where I sent you. And get it into your head – there's no way back from death.

After ten minutes in this place, Ursula is no longer thinking of the Tupamaros' escape, she isn't listening to Daddy, she isn't even thinking about the money. Her attention begins to focus on the rough floor, the walls closing in on them, her own exhaustion.

Her legs are trembling, her knees hurt, she alternates one hand with the other to hold the flashlight and support herself. As the physical pain is becoming the centre of her universe, the tunnel turns upwards.

Right now, she needs to focus all her efforts on the escape. *And on Luz's escape,* Daddy tells her, *because you are responsible for your sister's safety, you're the one who got her into this and you have to get her out, Ursula. Do you understand?*

For once in her life, Ursula doesn't argue.

Above the tunnel is Calle Solano García or perhaps even the garden of the house; she's not sure where they are because she doesn't know exactly how far they have gone. There are no reference points, the darkness has swept away any notion of space. The time that has elapsed is of no relevance because, contrary to our beliefs, time is not linear; and although our protagonists would swear they have been down there for hours, the entire sequence in the tunnel has taken place in a few short minutes. Ursula knows that when the tunnel turns uphill it is because they have reached the third stretch, and the end must be close. She feels more and more tired, and her hands and elbows are raw.

Both sisters are covered in mud and dust.

In the darkness, everything is different, Ursula thinks, and the pink bag that hangs from her shoulder grows heavier with each step. A lady's leather handbag, a cashmere cardigan, a wallet, an almost empty bottle of mineral water, a bundle of ten thousand dollars in thermo-sealed plastic – and a .38 revolver. An easy enough load to carry up there, in the daylight, but down here in this hole it has become a dead weight.

Ursula is on the verge of exhaustion. "I need to stop, Luz, I can't go any further."

"I don't want to stop. My phone battery is almost dead. I'm scared."

The torch is beginning to fade too, or at least that's how it seems.

The fear of being trapped in the belly of the earth propels them to keep going.

THE END

I

They finally glimpse some light when they are near the end, and they speed up despite their aching knees and their raw hands. The tiles covering the exit have been removed; the sisters are greeted by the gentle light that indicates they are inside a house, and by an instruction: "Arms first."

Hands reach out and pull them up through the narrow opening, and we cannot help thinking of corks popping out of a champagne bottle. First out is Luz; and she and Nico then extract Ursula.

The two women blink as their eyes adjust to the sudden brightness.

"And the owners of the house?"

"I told you, they're not here. They're on a winter vacation."

"So how did you get in?"

"I look after the house, it's a long story. I'll put back the tiles after you've gone. And the rug goes on top."

The women rub their knees, inspect the damage to their hands. Luz rubs her knuckles, her elbows. "Good. And the CCTV in the shopping mall?"

"The cameras on Level 0 had a technical fault, they stopped recording at exactly 15.01."

"Could anyone find out what caused it?"

"That would be difficult. It was a remote operation, via the Dark Web, the Onion Router. Do you know what that is?"

"Of course." Ursula nods and smiles, opens the wallet, takes out a bundle of green banknotes, offers it to the lad. "You deserve a break, Nico. Use this money to take the time to look for a job you actually enjoy. And could you look after this little thing until you hear from me?" She hands him the .38 and he puts it in his bag.

Then Luz and Ursula don long overcoats and sunglasses, and leave.

Nobody sees them come out, nobody recognizes them when they walk down a side street, away from a crowd of onlookers who are watching the comings and goings of the police and the special agents from behind the cordon.

They walk fast, turn left, take Calle Solano García south, then turn east onto Calle Guipúzcoa. They almost run the next two hundred yards. Ursula's car is parked on the next block.

Two women are waiting for them next to it.

"You're under arrest."

II

On a July evening, a car stops in a quiet street next to a high, gloomy wall. Inside, the four women are silent, until one of them opens the door.

"Here we are. Get out."

The four descend from the vehicle and walk to the entrance. They have an hour until it closes. Luz and Ursula have tangled hair, their faces are smeared with mud, their eyes are glazed, and the smell of soil, mould and death still clings to their nostrils. Despite the situation, they enjoy the caress of the cold sea breeze, so different from the stale air of the tunnel.

On the way from Punta Carretas, there was a heated discussion. Captain Leonilda Lima didn't beat around the bush, and accused Ursula of having taken part in the hold-up of the armoured truck and of having kept the money. Ursula asked what basis she had for her accusations. The captain replied that she didn't have any proof yet but she expected to soon, perhaps in minutes. Ursula went back on the offensive and asked if there was a warrant for their arrest. The captain shook her head and said she was sure she'd be able to get one if she called a magistrate. Ursula laughed, but the laughter sounded artificial and histrionic.

———

Jack is driving, Luz sitting next to her. The two women exchange glances, and Jack nods imperceptibly. Luz rewards the detective's silence with a flicker of a smile and a sigh of relief.

In the back are Ursula and Captain Leonilda Lima, one staring ahead with rage, the other with a triumphant tone.

"Let's talk about Antinucci, Ursula."

"What do you mean, 'let's talk'? Are you asking me something specific? If you want to arrest me, then ask me straightforward questions. If not, then wait for me to call a lawyer."

"I'm asking if you know him."

"Yes."

"How do you know him?"

"Is this an official interrogation?"

"You know it isn't."

"So why should I answer you?"

"Because in a few moments I'm going to prove that you were present at the attack on the armoured truck, that you have all the money, and that you shot Ricardo Prieto, alias the Hobo."

"Go on then, although I'm not sure how you intend to prove it." Ursula speaks in a calm, even tone, the statement sounding more like a question than a challenge.

Luz turns and looks at her; she sees something coldly calculating in her sister and looks away. Daddy was right, she thinks, Ursula's a black hole. She hears the captain speak again.

"How do I intend to prove it? You'll see."

"Where are you taking us?"

In the front seat, Luz and Jack look at each other without saying a word. The silence lasts for the rest of the journey.

The car draws up in a quiet street, in front of a high wall. "Here we are," Leonilda announces. "Get out."

III

The women get out of the car. They form a colourful group against the soot-stained perimeter wall, the wall that separates the dead from the living. Buceo Cemetery is close to the sea, on top of a hill.

"The cemetery: a very original place to take a suspect."

"Don't try to be funny, Ursula. We've only got an hour until it closes, so we'd better get a move on. Please take us to the family mausoleum, to where your father is." Leonilda hurries to correct herself. "To where your father's remains are."

Ursula's brow is furrowed, her expression uncertain, she is pale. If we could look inside her head, we would see anger and humiliation, and growing confusion. She swallows, shivers with the cold that doesn't allow her to think. The Indian summer is coming to an end.

Luz sees her shake her head; she takes Ursula by the arm and the two of them lead the way.

They go through a side gate, cross the central avenue and go down a minor path; they walk among cypresses and stone benches and funerary monuments of marble and granite. They don't talk to each other, don't look at each other.

———

Here, among the tombs, the dead are separated out into social classes, as they are in life: around the edges, against the walls, are the niches of the middle classes; in the centre, the mausoleums of wealthy families, the rich encased in coffins of oak and mahogany, in sepulchres sculpted from immortal stone. The privileged are assured that, just like their lives, their remembrance too will be nicer and will last longer.

Three workmen are repairing a tomb that is not exactly restrained. Corinthian columns sustain a pitched roof that shelters a floor of chequerboard tiles; three steps lead up to an iron door covered in verdigris, while a gallery of dour-faced sculptures looks on. The men are covering the walls with granite slabs. It seems that some people prefer to spend eternity in a building reminiscent of a bank.

Here, the only sounds are the noise of footsteps on gravel and the last birdsong of the day. There, surrounded by trees and the dead, the sweet smell of putrefaction speaks of interrupted projects, cancelled dreams, broken families. However, Buceo Cemetery is a good place to end one's existence; the grass is mowed regularly and is always green, many of the tombs have been built with skill, and some of them even offer a view of the sea. The women head east, distractedly checking the names above the gates of the mausoleums, some almost erased by wind and salt, by the passage of time, or because some of the letters have been stolen.

The tomb of the López family is at the end of a short path, close to the south wall; it is meticulously cared for: the metal is polished and the vases are full of fresh flowers. On the front, in letters of bronze, the name is clearly legible.

IV

The group halts.

The López mausoleum is made from light grey stone, colder, whiter, different in colour from the tombs that surround it. Leonilda looks up and observes the two angels which, from on high, stand guard over the bronze gate; they look down on the world and are armed with swords. These are not ornamental sculptures, she thinks, they are not there as decorations; they are intermediaries between the earth and the afterlife, they protect the residents of the tomb from evil spirits and also ensure that the souls of the departed do not return to torment the living. A shiver runs down her spine like a swarm of ants.

The bronze gate has a padlock.

"Open it, please. I know you've got the key."

It is the wrong thing to say. Ursula bites her lip, clenches her jaw, looks away. "I don't have it. I hope you don't think I carry the key to a mausoleum around with me."

"You might seem disturbed, Ursula, but I know you're also intelligent enough to realize it would be easy to get someone to open it up for me."

"You have no right to desecrate a tomb without a warrant."

The evening mist is spreading through the cypresses and the monuments. Ursula seems to be about to add something, but Luz interrupts. "I've got the key." The voice sounds distant, and it fades away into the silence. The evening light is waning.

Leonilda nods, holds out her hand. Luz takes out some keys, removes one from the bunch, hands it over.

The captain approaches the door, looks up at the guardian angels, shudders again. She thinks they look as if they are more interested in vengeance than in love or peace or justice. She swallows and hesitates before inserting the key. Finally, she turns the key and pushes the door.

Opening the door of a tomb is, in itself, a solemn act, and the sound of the rusty hinges surrounds it with a sinister, dramatic halo. From inside the tomb comes the crackle of dry leaves, a current of air heavy with the decades-old scent of mould, of earth, of rotten flowers. The air that emerges from the sepulchre is heavy with dust; it wafts around the four women, covers them, chokes them, blinds them. Ursula feels it in her face, as if something were flapping against her eyes, swatting her eyelids; she covers her face with her hands, opens her mouth, cries out in fear, then whispers: "Go away, Daddy, go away. Go back inside, don't come out. I'm begging you, please." She seems to be sobbing. She opens her eyes and looks as if she were in the presence of someone she knew, someone she had forgotten about and had then met again. "Go away, Daddy. I'm begging you, please." She stumbles backwards, blindly. Again, something flaps against her face and her clothes, sticks to her hair. She moves her arms and her hands like a sleepwalker, she shouts.

Leonilda once again feels the shudder running up her spine.

The dark air begins to dissipate: the moths twist and dance on the threshold, then the wind carries them away.

It is a moment before the four women speak.

Leonilda knows the relationship between the world and the netherworld, its secret laws, and it terrifies her; she feels an atavistic fear as she stands before this open tomb. She tries to recover her calm and looks suspiciously at the door: this is a passageway, an opening to another world. A black hole. The last moths are still emerging. She has to control herself and act, and do it now before it is too late. She bites her lips. "Ursula, I know you brought a suitcase to the cemetery. And it's in there, inside the mausoleum. Jacqueline followed you, she saw you go inside and hide it."

Ursula seems to be in a trance, catatonic, she gives no sign of having heard, she looks without seeing. Luz takes her sister by the shoulder, seeks out her eyes, interrogates her with her gaze. Ursula has an air of concern or of grief, as if the confusion of the moment has been joined by a sensation of imminent tragedy.

"Is what the captain says true? Did you bring a suitcase to the tomb? Why, Ursula? Why here?" Her voice is cracking.

"I brought it to Daddy. He told me that —"

"What did Daddy tell you?" Luz strokes her sister's hair, hugs her. "He's dead, my darling. He's dead."

Ursula rests her head on her sister's shoulder, closes her eyes, sinks into the embrace.

Leonilda decides to act; she pushes the door, then takes her hand away as if the door was hot or had an electric current running through it. She has a bad feeling. She wonders why she has involved herself in this. Some things are better left alone.

She has to draw on all her strength to keep going: she closes her eyes, and she sighs. She pushes the door all the way open, forces herself to take one step and then another. Inside the mausoleum, darkness reigns; it smells of melted wax, stagnant water, dead flowers. There are three coffins: one is elevated on a stand, the other two are parallel to it.

Leonilda's teeth are chattering, her hands are trembling, she rubs them together in an effort to cancel out the terror. But however hard she tries, she cannot contain her fear.

When her pupils become accustomed to the dark, she sees what she is looking for: the blue suitcase. It's at the back, in the corner, behind the coffins. The distance seems enormous.

She breathes in again. There's something evil about this place; Leonilda senses the threat and her hand reaches for the image of the Virgen Desatanudos, who protects us from the deceptions with which the Devil binds us.

The darkness and the perspective are misleading; the mausoleum is not so large and the suitcase is not so far away, just three or four paces, just three or four paces to get past the coffins. At first her legs don't respond, but she forces herself to follow a path between the dead, without looking at them. When she reaches the far wall, she takes the heavy suitcase by the handle and drags it back, past the dead again, to the door.

She emerges into the exterior and breathes. She leans against the wall, closes her eyes, inhales the pure air and waits until she has regained control of her limbs, until the trembling has stopped. She opens her eyes. Luz and Jack are observing her closely. Ursula, still clinging to Luz, is strangely distant, as if oblivious to it all.

The captain places the blue suitcase in front of Ursula. "Ladies. The money from the hold-up of the armoured truck is in here."

Ursula lets go of her sister and looks away. She shakes her head, mumbles. She grabs Luz's arm again. "Daddy told me to do it." Her words sound calm, but her hand grips her sister's arm like a vice.

"What have you done, Ursula? What made you want to hide it here, in the mausoleum?"

Ursula repeats the same litany, time and time again: Daddy told her, Daddy told her. And she presses her lips together in an expression that could signify determination or even fear.

Leonilda wants to get it over with, bring this absurd and dangerous situation to an end as soon as possible, get away from this sinister, evil place, and so she puts the suitcase on the grass and kneels. "Let's check what's inside the suitcase. Luz and Jacqueline, I'd like you to pay attention because you will be asked to give evidence as witnesses, to say what you saw inside it." Captain Lima undoes the zip and pulls back the lid in a rapid gesture, dramatic even, and reveals the contents.

The women look at the contents of the suitcase, then at each other.

It is 4.45 on a winter's evening in Montevideo. Beneath the cypresses and among the tombs there are more shadows than light.

The four pairs of eyes look once again at the contents of the blue suitcase: the Japanese figurines, the 322 figures made of ivory, porcelain, stone, wood; the princesses and opera singers and society ladies, the emperors and monks and warriors, the dogs and monkeys and rabbits.

Ursula looks at the suitcase, clenches her fists, looks up at the mausoleum. Her voice is deep and clear. "It's all here, Daddy. I never want to see them or you again."

Leonilda, who is kneeling in front of the suitcase, turns and looks at Ursula; her eyes are flashing with frustration, impatience and anger. When she talks she does so almost in a murmur. "The contents of this suitcase don't prove you didn't take part in the hold-up. I hope you don't think I'm stupid, Ursula, I know you were there. I know from witnesses that you were at the scene, that you shot the Hobo and made off with Diego and the money. I know you were with Antinucci in a garage close to your house and that you escaped. I'm sure you'd agree there are rather a lot of circumstances that link you to the robbery?"

Ursula takes a moment to react, she blinks, rearranges her hair, composes herself. She looks up, even smiles faintly. "I don't think you're stupid, captain, but I'm certain you have no way of proving what you've just said."

"Really? I'll tell you what I'm going to do. I'm going to order a paraffin test to confirm that there's powder residue on your hands, powder from the gun you used to shoot the Hobo. With that proof and the witnesses, we can charge you."

Ursula shakes her head again and looks at her in surprise. "Of course I've got powder residue on my hands."

"So you admit it."

Ursula looks up at the sky. A mass of white clouds passes overhead, from south to north. An ironic smile spreads across her face. "I admit to having powder on my hands."

"Thank you. That's all I wanted to know."

"I was at the San Juan celebrations a while ago, I let off rockets and bangers, fireworks. You know what it's like in Plaza Zabala…"

Leonilda interrupts her, speaking louder now, her voice echoing in the silence of the cemetery. "Do you think I'm going to believe that?"

"I'm not relying on your good faith. I have witnesses, my neighbours in the Old Town who were there that night. Go and look them up, like they do in the movies, when they find credible witnesses and discover the truth; show them a photo of me, ask them if they saw me that night. I mean, you know better than me what to do in these situations."

Jack, who had been inspecting the guardian angels without missing a word of the exchange, turns and takes two steps, and stands in front of Leonilda. "That won't be necessary. I was in the square that night, Leonilda, and I saw Ursula and it's like she says, she was letting off fireworks. There's no need to do all the stuff they do in the movies, because I was there too."

"Like I said, captain, I have gunpowder on my hands and arms. And a good explanation." She looks at the police officer, who lowers her gaze, lost in thought.

The evening has turned orange and then grey; in a few minutes, night will have fallen.

Leonilda bites her lower lip, smiles at the woman standing in front of her. Her frustration seems to be dissipating and there is a brief intimacy, perhaps even a certain empathy that may reflect her attempt to return to a less dramatic reality or that could simply be the result of exhaustion at the end of a long day. "You win, Ursula."

"If you don't mind me making a suggestion, why don't you investigate the lawyer? He's not exactly straight."

"Antinucci? Unless I'm mistaken, the lawyer visited you at home just a few days ago."

"I see you're well informed, captain."

"I'll certainly carry on investigating him. And now we're on the subject, I can tell you that at least for the next few days he's going to be under guard and out of circulation."

"Jesus, that's a surprise. And why might that be?"

"After you left the shopping mall, the lawyer and his side-kick were arrested by the police because of the shots fired. The charges won't be anything serious: disturbing public order, illegal possession of firearms, endangering public safety, nothing that would earn you a serious punishment in this country. They'll be out in a few days, I should imagine."

"Our lawyer, under arrest. Who would have thought it, a man with all those contacts. Do you think there really is such a thing as justice?" There is no response, just a silence that continues until Ursula brings it to a close. "I see."

"Can I ask you a question, Ursula?"

"I reserve the right to remain silent."

"How did you manage to escape from the mall? How did you manage to vanish into thin air? All the exits were under surveillance and nobody saw you."

Ursula tosses her head back and looks Leonilda up and down.

Leonilda sees a woman who is beautiful if a little over-weight. Her light brown hair comes down to her shoulders, she has a broad, smooth forehead, her mouth is a little wider than the one that will feature in the identikit photo she will concoct tonight, aided by her own memory and by a recent but very grainy photograph, taken from a distance and from above.

The unanswered questions seem destined to multiply this evening at Buceo Cemetery.

Captain Lima observes the two sisters, switching from one face to the other, thinking that one is a criminal and the other an accessory, but who among us is not one of these things at some point in our life? And she is so tired.

"We'll meet again, I'm sure, Ursula." Then she sighs and there even seems to be a possibility she will shout out in protest against the relentless failure of her life. But she surrenders to the disappointment, yet another disappointment.

She and Jack turn and leave without saying goodbye.

V

As they watch them go down the gravel path, Ursula checks the time. "I have to go."

"Are you going home?"

"I'm leaving Montevideo, I have to get out of the country for a while."

"Right now?"

"I've got some unfinished business with someone who's in hospital. I'll deal with it and then I'll go."

"Take care, Ursula."

"Will you look after the mausoleum, look after Daddy and Mummy and Auntie Irene?"

Luz sighs, and promises with her eyes. "Of course, my dear."

"And my money. You need to go and get it right now and put it somewhere safe. You'll have to hide it."

"Just tell me what to do."

"Go down to the basement, let yourself into the elevator shaft with this little key. There's no need to be afraid, it hasn't worked for months and there isn't a single replacement motor in the whole country. At the side, in the dark, there's a blue suitcase. Inside it are my millions, and my partner's too. Will you do that for me?"

"You know I will, I always do what you ask." Luz puts the keys in her pocket.

"In a few days I'll send you a message from a telephone abroad. It will have the name and number of a bank account in Switzerland."

Luz nods.

"Don't forget to lock the door of the mausoleum."

Luz shakes her head. "And the figurines?"

"They're Daddy's. I gave them back. It took me all of this to understand him. I don't think I'll see him again."

The sisters hug; Luz kisses Ursula on the cheek. "I know it sounds banal, but take care."

They separate, and Ursula walks off, picking her way through gravestones and sculptures.

"Ursula, did you kill Auntie Irene?"

Ursula walks away, a smile on her lips, which are slightly parted as she savours the night air; she answers without turning her head. The faintest of voices reaches Luz's ears. "Yes, I killed her." Ursula doesn't stop, doesn't wait for the next question. Her smile grows wider and she continues on her way through the trees and the benches and the monuments.

Luz buttons up her coat and raises her collar; the wind is getting colder. She touches the bunch of keys in her pocket, takes them out and inspects them. She shakes her head. She'll go today, she'll take care of everything. She raises her voice a little louder. "And Daddy?"

Her sister can't hear her now, she has disappeared among the cypresses and the graves, has vanished into the mist and the twilight. Who knows what the future holds?

Author's Note

Then, as now, Uruguay was a small country but one with pretensions. The three million or so inhabitants call it *el paisito*, the little country, with false modesty and evident pride. And to illustrate our glorious past, we like to recount how it became known as the "Switzerland of South America". This epithet – coined by a US journalist in the early twentieth century, used and abused by the leaders of successive governing parties, proclaimed to the four winds, repeated a thousand and one times over the years until it was engraved in the collective subconscious – now clashes head-on with a very different reality, one a long way from the Europeanizing optimism of the original comparison. But Uruguayans, citizens of a country that has known better days, refuse to let go of this view of our country as an island of exceptionalism in a sea of injustice, illegality, ignorance and crime. As we sip our coffee, pass round the *mate* or savour a glass of Tannat wine, we boast of our country's historic achievements in social and educational rights, we brandish some positive contemporary statistics – the high regard for democracy, the atheism or secularism of our institutions – and, of course, we recall old triumphs on the soccer field. If our companions appear unimpressed by the list of these achievements, if they are unmoved by this rosary of exceptions, then we bring up a fact that, at least for a time, earned our country a place in the *Guinness Book of Records*: Operation El Abuso.

It was 1971 and, although the dictatorship had not yet come to power, it was already waiting in the wings. "El Abuso" was the slyly humorous code name given by those who masterminded it to the breakout of more than a hundred political prisoners from Punta Carretas Prison shortly before the military dictatorship took over. Epic, incredible, cinematographic, the operation freed 111 political inmates, including the leaders of the Movimiento de Liberación Nacional-Tupamaros, striking a blow at the government and stunning the entire country. The newspapers, with black and white photos, recount how, on 6 September, Uruguayans awoke to dramatic news of the escape from Punta Carretas Prison (a high-security jail built at the start of the twentieth century and located not far from the city centre), an establishment that had already had its five minutes of fame in 1931 when a group of eight anarchists and three fellow prisoners tunnelled their way out.

In the 1971 jailbreak, the prisoners filed through bars, drilled through cement, dug through the earth, made lanterns, propped and ventilated the passageway and constructed a fifty-yard tunnel that led from cell 73, on the ground floor, passed below Calle Solano García and emerged in a private residence. That morning, the owners of the house watched as more than a hundred people emerged through a hole in the floor measuring twenty inches by twenty-four. An hour after the escape they alerted the police, who didn't believe them until an inspection revealed numerous empty cells, and a head count confirmed that 111 of the jail's inmates were absent. Astonishingly, the engineering work to dig the tunnel had gone unnoticed, and the escape itself took place without a single shot being fired. After this, the government called on the army to intervene in the fight against the armed groups, and it may be around this time that the notorious Órgano Coordinador de Operaciones Antisubversivas was created and tasked with repressing the opposition.

Many years later, after democracy had been re-established, several of the guerrillas who had escaped through the tunnel came to occupy positions in government. One of the escapees, José "Pepe" Mujica, was elected president in 2009, while another, Eleuterio Fernández Huidobro, became Minister of Defence in 2011.

Nine years after the end of the dictatorship, a shopping mall was built on the site of the prison. "We prefer not to identify with the prison, although we have maintained some of its architectural elements," explained one of the developers of Punta Carretas Shopping, who added, "Our idea was always to associate the shopping mall with freedom and traditional values. We have transformed a prison into a space of complete freedom." Former president, José "Pepe" Mujica, offers a different view: "This was a monument to pain and monotony, and today it has a festive appearance. The same stones but with different paint."

In the centre itself, there is no trace of the Tupamaros' tunnel, no reference to Operation El Abuso, nothing to recall what was one of the most important jailbreaks in history. Part of our *paisito*'s past has been erased.